LET THE LITTLE BIRDS SING

Let the Little Birds Sing

Sandra Fox Murphy

atmosphere press

Enjoy the Spring of Love and Youth,
    To some good angel leave the rest;
For Time will teach thee soon the truth,
    There are no birds in last year's nest!

~ Henry Wadsworth Longfellow

CHAPTER 1

The snow began to fall as we stood before the pit in the ground by the leafless maple, my hand held tight in my mother's. Pa, Grandma, and Grandpa stood with us as the pastor read from his worn Bible, frayed by years of turning pages.

> *"Let there be, sayeth the Lord, a time for everything, and a season for every activity under the heavens; a time to be born and a time to die, a time to plant and a time to uproot.*
>
> *"And...then shall the dust return to the earth as it was: and the spirit shall return unto God who gave it."*
>
> *Lord, in heaven, we pray you take our sweet Hester into your arms and give comfort to the mother whose arms are now empty. Amen.*

The words were a blur to my ears, for my eyes were set on the tiny coffin in the black hole, so deep the winter sun couldn't find it. When the prayers were done, the last amen said, Pa threw a handful of dirt that landed with a thud on the wooden box that held my baby sister, and the sound of it startled me. Ma sobbed quietly, and Uncle Levi used the shovel to begin filling the grave in the ground not yet frozen. I snuggled tight into my mother's faded blue coat for both warmth and comfort.

My five-year-old sister Emily was at the church with the women. Together we walked away, back toward the church, leaving baby Hester alone in the graveyard, a place I'd always seen as mysterious and lonely. A place with shadows that trembled as if the dead struggled to return. Ma's hand gently drew my head to rest at her waist as she walked with the heaviness of the baby to come, and snowflakes began to drift from the dark gray clouds, dusting our coats and skirts into ghostly hues.

"Mama, will the new baby stay with us?"

Ma looked down at me. It was a moment before a fragile smile betrayed her sad eyes.

"Oh, dear Fidelia, I hope so. I hope so," she said and then looked up toward the sky, where the snow caressed her face.

Just two weeks later Maureen was born.

When May blossomed in Indiana, the storms came with the daily afternoon gathering of dark clouds that dumped their bounty and left as quickly as they'd arrived. Grandpa had decided we should head south, where it was warmer, where there were not so many new German immigrants from the East growing the nearby towns, and where the sky was said to be tall and wide. Over the years, beginning long before I was born, the Indian tribes had been moved farther and farther to the west, accommodating the white man's settlement. I had heard Grandpa's stories of how he had fought the Indians under Colonel Harrison's command, and now only the Miami tribe remained, and they were being sent, bit by bit, to Kansas. Tensions in Indiana were growing regarding the presence of Negro families settling from the South, and I had heard Ma and Pa whisper of the good works of the Underground Railroad and the Quakers.

It was the year 1847, the beginning of our long journey. I was only seven then, when I helped Ma pack the wagon. Pa said we were all leaving for a place far away called Texas. Across the field I could see Pa's sister, Audrey, and younger brother, Jeremy, walking to and fro Grandpa's wagon. Pa and Grandpa had sown no crops that year, but the white wildflowers and some early bright milkweed were springing up in the meadows. Beyond, in my uncle's fields, I could see the tiniest sprigs of corn stalks escaping the turned dirt. Jeremy and Audrey were going to Texas with us. Grandma had been the only grandmother I'd known because Ma's mother, Grandmother Mariah, had lived in Ohio and had died before my memories were formed. Ma was named Mariah after her own mother. Grandpa William, my pa's father, had been born in Ohio but had come to Fort Wayne with his family as a young child, had grown up on the farm amidst the goings and comings of the nearby fort.

I'd heard conversations at our supper table, talk about why we had to leave Indiana. Ma was anxious about leaving a place she'd come to love, leaving behind her sister.

"Mariah, it's what Father wants, and I can't argue with him. We can get more land in Texas. Someone came back from some part of Texas and told Father about the vast fields of cotton . . . how much profit came from the man's own crops," said Pa.

"But, John, most years our crops flourish. And we have family here. And in Ohio," said Ma, her words and imploring voice seeking to change Pa's decision.

"First of all, I don't want Father going to this new land without me. I, too, would like a grand farm, and I'm certain the new markets in the pioneer settlements will welcome availability of more goods and produce," said Pa. He took Ma's hand across the table. "We will be better for this, Mariah."

Ma's face did not reflect the reassurance given her.

As we packed our things, I thought of little Hester, only fifteen months old when her life was snatched, now in the cold field that will be covered with snow next winter, after we are gone. Back in those years, when I was seven, I did not know better. I wondered if she would miss us. If she would be warm enough when the snows came again.

There was only so much room in our wagon, so we chose our most special things to take, things that we would need, and left behind what we could do without. Our land and farmhouse would go to my uncle. Ma talked Pa into taking her favorite soft chair, and it now sat in the back of our big wagon like a sanctuary in a thick forest, its pale blue velvet tempting respite. Ma's chair would prove to be a soft spot for me and Emily during the weeks to come, and where Ma would often nurse our new sister.

I packed my chemises and dresses in a chintz bag Ma had sewn for me. The chintz was dressed in a cheerful pattern of blackbirds and red flowers and grasses sprinkled with yellow buttercups and some butterflies. After my bag was packed, I packed Emily's clothes in the bag Ma had sewn for her, the one with bluebirds and purple asters. Emily had just turned five in December, and then there was our newest sister, Maureen, just a tiny baby. Every time I turned around Ma had Maureen at her breast, so, being the oldest, I helped Ma pack up the kitchen. The grains and dried turkey, along with Ma's best pans, would go into the chuck wagon, still sitting across the field at Grandpa's house.

I carried Emily's and my satchels to Ma in the wagon, where Ma was folding blankets and dresses, hanging a few to wear.

"Fidelia, help me here. Let's make some places to sleep by stacking the blankets. And then you can help me carry my spinning wheel over there, in the back," said Ma.

"Pa's putting all the horse food in the small wagon," I said.

"Well, they can put their tools and tobacco in there too. Fidelia, go ask your pa for all the bed rolls. We'll put them in here."

Finally, on a sunny morning, after all goodbyes had been said, I sat next to Ma on the wagon seat, holding the baby. Emily was sitting in the blue chair in the back of the wagon, her eyes fluttering into sleep. The night before, Ma had hugged her own sister, Uncle Levi's wife, long and hard, not knowing when or if she would see her again. When all was readied and Ma had snapped the reins, the wagon jerked forward, and I turned to see my cousin Jane running alongside us.

"I love you, Fidelia," she yelled.

Ma waved at her. "We love you too, dear Jane," Ma called back, and I waved and saw my cousin fall back behind us and turn to walk home, her head bent low. I tried hard to print the image of her in my head to remember later. Her long yellow curls, like Emily's, and her cheeks always pinked by the sun. A little taller than my sister. I played this vision of Jane over and over in my head to assure I would not forget.

We were the second wagon in what Grandma called a train, with the chuck wagon behind us and Grandpa riding his horse. Uncle Jeremy, a young man of nineteen with a twitch that came and went aside his eye, held the reins of the lead wagon with Grandma sitting next to him. Pa drove the chuck wagon, led by the two oxen, with two extra horses tied behind it. At that moment, it seemed a new world was before us, but it would not be long before I felt like I had traveled the world and beyond. No one had told me Texas was so far.

That first night we stopped at the side of the trail, amidst a copse of trees with a nearby creek, and Emily and I watched Ma and Grandma fix a meal at the chuck wagon. Unbeknownst to Emily and me, this would be our life, repeated over and over, for many weeks to come. On that first night we ate beans with biscuits and turkey, and Ma made a pot of coffee. When Ma wasn't watching, I stole a sip from her cup. I had always loved the scent of Ma's coffee that brewed on the old iron stove, but when the hot liquid first hit my tongue I was startled by its bitterness. I would, however, sneak more sips in the future and, over time, would come to love the hot drink. On that first night, when the moon was full and shone amidst the illumined clouds, Ma and I rearranged the bedding in our wagon, where we slept while the men bedded down near the waning campfire. It seemed an adventure to me and to Emily as we, so close together, giggled in a strange place where the stars shone above.

After several days we came to a large river, the Mississippi, at a town called Chester. Pa called it the Chester Crossing, and the men drove our wagons right onto this large, flat boat that took us down and across the river to the other side. My eyes were big as saucers as we rode the water, with Emily squeezing my hand, and I can say, looking back now, that I was fearful as we all floated on that fast-moving river where the water looked menacing. Like a monster to a naïve seven-year-old girl. Emily held tight to me and, at times, I felt the shake of her head as she cried with the jagged sway of the boat. Once safe on the other side, relief wide in my sister's eyes, our wagons continued on through the Missouri territory, west and then south toward the mountains.

"We will wind through the Ozarks, the mountains just south of us. The barge captain, at Chester, told me to take the big road out of Springfield," said Grandpa at the campfire one night. "There'll be plentiful game down there, John."

"There will be games?" I asked Pa.

"No, Fidelia. Game means prey. Grandpa and I will be able to hunt some fresh turkey and rabbit for stew," said Pa.

"Oh," I replied, looking toward the flames in the fire and thinking of the poor rabbit. I remembered Ma making rabbit stew in Indiana. That night Pa slept in the wagon with us, and baby Maureen snuggled between Emily and me. Before I fell asleep, I heard Ma sighing deep, over and over, and I wondered what she fretted over, but it would be many years from that night before I would understand the sighs I heard from Ma. Before dawn, the baby startled us awake with her demand for Ma's breast, and I carried her to where Ma slept.

We traveled for weeks on end through mountains and plains in the rains and brutal sun, and I can assure you that, being so young, I had no concept of time and surely none of the grand distances that lay between territories and people, people so different I could never have imagined. As we traveled through Missouri, the landscape changed and the hills grew, and over the years before me, I would change and grow as well.

"This Springfield Trail takes us to Arkansas, is that true?" asked Pa of a hunter standing in front of Springfield's General Store, where Ma and Grandma were buying supplies.

"Yah, sir. That would be the way," said the hunter, his rifle slung over his shoulder. "There's some rough parts along the way, and you may have to double-team your wagons to get up some grades. Down the road you will cross the James River and later on, as you near Arkansas, the White. Beware the White River. The trail, the Springfield Road, was an old Indian trail, and you'll likely run into a few of 'em. Most are harmless."

"Thank you, sir," said Pa. "Is there a ferry at the James River?"

"Nope."

Pa lifted me up onto the seat of our wagon.

"Wait here for Ma," he said. Pa walked toward Grandpa, shared a few words, then entered the store. I sat on the wagon seat and Emily played inside the wagon, where the baby slept.

When the rains fell along the trail we needed to stop, if it poured hard, to avoid the gullies where the water would run wild, and on those days, we barely made it ten or fifteen miles. On one great rise into the mountains, Pa had to take the wagons up one at a time, with double the oxen, then lead the oxen back down the long hill to hitch another wagon. The day was pretty much done when all the wagons were at the hilltop as we anticipated the steep descent to come. Over the coming weeks, this process would repeat at too many places, slowing our journey and maddening Pa.

Looking back from passed time, I believe that is when my pa began to lose faith. Those slow and brutal climbs through the mountains, and all that would come after. I remember the change of Pa's posture that revealed, for me, the beginning of the change in him.

I shall never forget the foggy day on that trail when I saw my first black bear, lumbering through the trees near our wagon and vanishing into the cover of the brush. Emily squealed, but my heart sang at once with both glee and fright.

Many nights of camping through the woods and hills of the Ozark Mountains lay before me. As I, now a young woman with a child of my own, share this story with you, my memories are recorded and clear in my mind, as if I'm living them again.

CHAPTER 2

Falling. I was falling. Then spinning, a sharp pain in my jaw as it hit something wooden, some part of the wagon. Pain burned through my head, my neck. Burning pain. Falling, over and over, within the canvas as I heard the screams of Emily, my ma's cries seeming so far away. When it all stopped, there was a momentary silence and then the rustling of blankets and the thumps of boxes tumbling into place, and I lay still, hesitant, unsure of where I was. I saw the spinning wheel upside down, the wooden wheel cracked open. Then there was the sound of Pa and Grandpa running through brush, calling our names. The sound of Ma, distant, weeping.

We had been in the hills of Missouri, the Ozarks, for almost a week, and on this particular day, the sky was gray, dark, near the color of night, and the rain pounded down relentlessly. We had not traveled far that morning, and I remember wondering when Grandpa would tell us to stop. I had been standing under the canvas, just behind Ma, whose skirt was dripping water that pooled and fell from the foot box. I watched the wagon in front struggle in the mud when I was abruptly thrown forward and my own fall began. Ma had yanked the reins when the mud pulled at the wheels, throwing me off balance, and the wagon had swayed and leaned too far to the right, throwing Ma into the sludge before the wagon had tumbled toward the woods.

Grandpa pulled me out of the broken wagon, and Pa climbed in amidst the chaos. Grandpa sat me down on the ground as Pa handed Maureen to Grandpa. The baby was crying; she would stop wailing and then start again as though she was uncertain of the fitting response to an unfamiliar event.

"The baby looks fine, Father. I think she bounced around like a ball wrapped in all those blankets," said Pa.

Maureen lay whimpering in Grandpa's lap, catching her breath as he turned his attention toward me. "Stand up, Fidelia, if you can. Let me see your face," he said.

I stood as I saw Pa climb back into the wagon as we heard my sister Emily's wails. She had fallen to the back of the wagon. Grandpa touched my face. It smarted, diverted my attention away from my sister's well-being. The rains had not stopped in the midst of the commotion, but the coolness of raindrops felt like a healing balm on my wounded jaw.

"It's just a scrape. I think your face will swell from the jolt. Your ma will put something on it, but it will heal fine. Open your mouth. Let me see your teeth."

I opened wide and he checked my teeth.

"Spit, Fidelia. In the grass."

I spit and saw blood.

"You may have cracked a tooth. But a new one will come in later. If I have to, I'll pull it."

I spit again, but there was little blood, and I hoped, gathering all my wishes into one, that Grandpa would not have to pull any teeth.

Pa squirmed out of the wagon with one arm while he held Emily with the other. She was still crying.

"I think she's broke her arm," yelled Pa.

"Grandma will know how to set it, Emily. How to fix it so it will heal," explained Grandpa. The horses struggled to get up from their harnesses still held by the yoke of the wagon. Their struggle was a good sign. The hitch held them in place as they thrashed and, likely, the horses had kept the wagon from falling farther down the hill. That, and the large sycamore pressing into the canvas. Grandpa handed the baby to me.

"John, lay Emily here on my lap and take the baby up to her ma. We'll be here for a day or two, if not more. Tell Jeremy to find a spot nearby to set camp, to cut some brush away, if need be."

Grandpa shook his head back and forth as Pa struggled up the wet hill with the baby. "What a mess," Grandpa said.

He looked at Emily, at the bend of her arm, and flinched. I ran my hand over Emily's head as she sobbed, trying to comfort her as we waited for Pa to come back, and then we all stumbled up the hill to the trail as Grandpa carried my sister.

"I'll go back down and get the horses," said my pa to Grandpa. He turned down the hill, his foot slipping out from under him in the wet grass, and he slid down the embankment into the gray mare. Grandpa told Uncle Jeremy to wait on moving the wagons and sent him to help Pa with the horses, and I found Ma was still crying as Grandma carried Emily to her wagon.

"Stop it, Mariah. It was not your fault. It could a' happened to any of us in all this mud. And Emily will be fine," said Grandma in her terse way of trying to calm her daughter-in-law. My grandma was an earnest woman, abiding little nonsense, especially from the men folk, I noticed. But don't misunderstand. Grandma always took care of all of us.

I followed Ma, and I could hear my sister's soft cries as I surrendered to the rain dripping from my chin and the muddy water soaking the hem of my dress, washing away the moments of a luckless day.

As the rain pelted the canvas, Emily lay sleeping on a stack of blankets. Grandma had moved Emily's arm in such a way that made her scream and set to sobbing again. The exhaustion of the pain and weeping carried her to sleep. A wrapping of linens was on her arm now, making it difficult for her to move it as the rain persisted through the day, ceasing just in time for supper. No one was in a good humor.

After the wagons were moved, Grandma set up the campfire and pots under a tree, but we still had to tromp through the mud to the chuck wagon. Our supper prayers gave thanks to God that no one was killed or maimed in the accident. The gray skies made the mood somber; however, Grandpa was always a storyteller, and in spite of our low spirits, or perhaps because of such, he began one of his tales.

"When I was boy, just barely out of short pants, I knew a fella at the fort near our farm," he said. "He was an Indian agent, with the War Department, and spent years documenting the words of the Ottawa. Journals and journals of Indian words. He would show them to me, and I would try to utter the words, but was certain an Indian would never understand me. This agent, a diligent man, an

Irishman, come to Indiana through Pennsylvania. Smarter than I knew I'd ever be, but I learned a lot from that Mister Johnston. Over the years, it's served me well in my own dealings with the Indians."

"What's an Indian agent?" I asked Grandpa.

"An Indian agent is a man chosen to talk with the Indian tribes, to bargain with them on behalf of the government. When I was just seventeen the government sent Mister Johnston to Ohio."

"Why?"

"Don't know for sure, but I suspect they thought he was getting too friendly with the natives."

After our accident, Pa had to put one of the horses down when she couldn't get up, her leg shattered by the fall. I was grateful that they didn't have to shoot Emily. It was the gray mare Pa had to put down, and now there would be only one spare horse behind the chuck wagon on the trail to Texas. I overheard that our wagon, once pulled back to the trail, would need a wheel fixed, repairs to the wagon bed, and a new frame formed for the canvas. Grandpa said it would be at least two days before we were moving again. The women and children all piled into Grandma's wagon for the night and the men slept beneath the wagons for shelter from the rains that came and left all night, and we awoke in the morning to find the sun shining.

After gathering six fresh eggs from the coop affixed to the chuck wagon, I helped Ma make breakfast while the men fed the horses. With breakfast finished, the work began. Aunt Audrey and I carried small items from inside the fallen wagon, trudging uphill as Pa and Jeremy worked on the broken wheel. As Grandpa stood near the chuck wagon cutting strips from a felled pine, I saw a man, his head covered in fur, lead his horse from the darkness of the woods. Behind him came an Indian man, taller than I thought an Indian would be, his face harsh from either age or sun, and there was gray amidst the black of his long, braided hair. The Indian man wore no shirt, and I could see that he was thin yet strong. He led a beauty of a pinto horse without a saddle, followed by a packhorse loaded with bundles and tethered to the pinto.

"Grandpa! Grandpa, there's someone coming behind you," I called.

He turned to see the two men approaching him. I saw Grandpa's hand hover over the gun at his hip.

"Friendly, sir," yelled the mustached man with the furry hat. "*Bonjour*. We are friends. Only trappers." He raised his free hand to remove his hat and waved as if showing he meant no harm, held no weapons.

And that is how we came to meet Edmund Francois Chouteau and his companion, Gray Feather.

CHAPTER 3

Pa was wary of this character Edmund and his friend, but Grandpa, being Grandpa, welcomed them to our campfire to share in our next meal. As I recalled from Grandpa's stories of his youth in Fort Wayne, he had been no stranger to the fur trade. William McCord, my grandpa, had not had an easy childhood, helping his own father with farms in Ohio, then in Indiana, where the family was often called to ward off Indian attacks. Yet, as treaties were signed in the new territories, Grandpa told us stories of Indians he had befriended when he was a young farmer in Indiana. Once he told us of a young Miami man, not much more than eighteen, whom he had found fallen in the forest. He brought the injured man home to his young wife, Mary, my grandma, and she nursed the man's wounds. In return, the once-painted warrior, called Sitting Hawk by the Miami tribe, stayed through a season to help with Grandpa's harvest. Once the crops were gathered, he vanished.

"I'm certain, in battle, this warrior, covered with most delicate lines of ink on his skin, would have sent me to my death, but in coming to know him, I found a sense of honor I find in few white men," Grandpa had shared at the supper table one evening back in Indiana. I knew my grandpa had a respect for the much-feared native people and would welcome Gray Feather.

Some of Grandpa's stories were about the trappers, colorful characters who traded at the fort. These men, from both the West and the North, plied their furs to new settlers seeking the warmth and quality of their goods. Grandpa said these men seemed fearless and that we would learn, soon enough, that Edmund was no different.

Edmund was handsome, with a friendly smile . . . like the furriers Grandpa always described, he exuded a zealous spirit and shared colorful stories of encounters in the mountains and escapades in St. Louis. I could not help but wonder as he shared his stories around the campfire, so animated, if these were fairy tales or outright lies, but nevertheless, he had us all spellbound. Jeremy listened with deep interest, clearly having a grand awe of Edmund Chouteau and his adventures. My young uncle had often spoken to me about his dreams of heading west, of seeing the world, daydreaming as he hoed weeds from rows and rows of corn in Indiana.

In contrast to Edmund, Gray Feather seldom spoke, and I saw my pa often eyeing this fellow. The Indian held stoic, his emotions unrevealed or absent, but I saw something in his eyes. It wasn't a twinkle, but maybe it was. I could not quite tell, but his silent deliberation entranced me. As did his looks. His leggings were buckskin, as was the tunic he put on before our meal; beads were sewn on the sleeves and one dark gray feather hung from the leather band holding his braided hair. As I watched Mister Edmund, I saw that his fancy gestures and speech were sprinkled with French words that I did not understand. His hair was dark, almost black, and hung in waves to his shoulders, and there was the hint of a chiseled jaw beneath his bearded growth. Mister Edmund's handsome appearance, coupled with his charm, belied a gentleman who was, as Mama would say, carefree.

"My friend here, Gray Feather, is an excellent tracker," said Edmund. "I would not have near the number of bundles on that packhorse were it not for the skills and prowess of my Osage friend. He has been with me since my first year of trapping, when I was merely eighteen. *Mon meilleur ami.*"

We all looked at Gray Feather. He said nothing but remained stone-faced.

"Only *la vieille* . . . um, *comment on dit*? . . . yesterday, he spotted the scat of an elk, and we followed the scattered trail in the moss. Just over the hill I saw the grandest elk I'd ever seen. There were three does and a calf I imagine birthed in the spring, and a grand antlered stag. My vision could not leave the stag's majesty . . . but then we moved on, for I do not hunt elk," said Edmund. "Yet that scene is engraved in my mind and will probably stay for a time to come."

Emily and I sat side by side, our eyes wide and, I imagine, our jaws gaping. But Edmund continued.

"I must share how Gray Feather came to be my partner. My own father, Francois, traded with the Osage along the Missouri River, and that is how Gray Feather came to be my friend. But before that, before I was even born, my grandfather, Auguste Chouteau of St. Louis, born in New Orleans, lived with an Osage tribe when he was young and later became an Indian agent. In our history lies a great esteem between the Chouteau and the Osage."

"I am impressed, Mister Chouteau, just as I have known a couple of Indian agents in Indiana, as well as exuberant fur trappers," said Grandpa.

"If you would allow, Mister McCord, tomorrow Gray Feather and I can help you to lift that wagon from the ravine."

"No need," said Pa swiftly.

"We would be grateful for such help, friend," said Grandpa in a more measured and kindly tone. "I suspect we shall need your help getting that damned thing back on the trail. And, please, you may call me William."

Pa's expression was one of frustration, not eager to have these characters stay among us.

"*Merci* for your gracious welcome, friends. Bid you *bon nuit*. Gray Feather and I will camp in the trees nearby, as we are accustomed," said Edmund as he and Gray Feather rose to leave. I watched Edmund nod toward Aunt Audrey before he turned to go.

Work began early the next morning, at dawn. The five men struggled to get the shattered wagon upright. They had already removed the broken wheel. Because the grass had dried over the past day, they decided to hitch the three strongest horses to help pull the wagon up.

The young roan skittered. The memory of the wagon's fall remained with the horse, and Gray Feather held back as Pa began to bridle the team. I walked over to the roan, and he neighed and jumped with my approach. I knew this horse well as I'd ridden on him with Pa at our farm, and I was not afraid of his restiveness for I knew it was he who was fearful. I stood to his rear as his front quarters hit the ground, and it was then that I took his rein firmly in my hand, but not too taut.

"Erie," I whispered his name. "Erie." I stroked his neck, and as he began to calm, I stroked his face.

"Delia. Let your pa do that," yelled Grandma.

That is when Gray Feather took over. He gently whistled for the roan to come to him toward the ravine, where Pa would need to add Erie to the yoke and then descend to the fallen wagon. I let the rein go and he went to Gray Feather. The Indian held the rein loosely and spoke to the horse in whispered words I could not hear. It was apparent, immediately, that the Indian had a way with horses.

After the team was hitched to the wagon, I saw Gray Feather speak in that same soft sound to the two mares and the gelded roan, and then he slowly led them up the hill as Edmund, Pa, and Uncle Jeremy guided the remains of the wagon from behind. The wagon finally sat, forlorn, at the side of the trail. The men decided they wouldn't upright it until the hitch and the wheel were mended and on the wagon. As the men worked on the repairs through the day, the women quickly patched the tears in the wagon's canvas.

It appeared we would be on the move the following day, or perhaps the day beyond, but tension arose in the camp as my sweet Aunt Audrey had caught the eye of charming Edmund. Audrey was only seventeen, the youngest child of my grandparents, but she had a whimsical nature and was quite a beauty. The Irish traits had all come together at her birth, for she had delicate, fair skin framed by wild red hair, her eyes an ice blue that seemed to pierce into the depths of another world. I did not acquire such features, but instead the dark hair and hazel eyes of my own mother. Heads turned when Aunt Audrey walked into a room, and her beauty had not escaped the attention of the French trapper. I was not too young then to wonder if this handsome young man had a wife and children housed far away as I often spied him eyeing my aunt. Aunt Audrey would swoon and flirt in conversation with the trapper. She was plainly smitten with the Frenchman.

"This land, the Ozarks, is laid *superbe* in the white of winter. The trees cascade on the hills spired toward the sky, sparkling with white ice, the ground covered in deep snow, *majestueux* . . . and all the better to find the beavers, the rabbits. Well, perchance not the white ones. Easier than now, in the spring," said Edmund as we finished our evening meal near the chuck wagon. He looked toward Audrey. "It is a good thing, with all my time in these mountains with Gray Feather, that I have not a wife, nor children, waiting alone, afar, for my return."

Well, so he said, I thought. How was I to know his words were true, and I saw the grimace on Pa's face.

"That is God's truth," said Pa. "No woman would fancy such a lonely life."

Edmund smiled, looking towards Pa. "*Vrai*. True words. But I am certain the day shall come that a woman will capture my heart, a woman who, with a spirit a bit wild, will change my wandering ways."

It was at that moment that I saw Gray Feather, always stoic, grin. I could not interpret the meaning of his countenance, but the tension amongst the group turned palpable, and the air grew heavy. Audrey blushed.

"Well, Audrey, let us clean these dishes," said Grandma, and the women rose to gather the plates. It had not gone unnoticed by me that Aunt Audrey was lovesick. She was clearly entranced by this handsome and eccentric man in our midst, spellbound by his words. As I recall that first night he took a meal with us, she had quietly watched Mister Edmund, with marvel in her eyes, and on this night, I heard her giggling in a way I had not heard before, her cheeks pink. I could not help but wonder what would come of this when, in a day to two, we would go our separate ways.

CHAPTER 4

I awoke early the next morning and found the skies gray, threatening more rain, as I wandered among the tall poplar trees to find a spot to ease myself. There was a breeze and I was drawn to the sound of songbirds, the clear whistle of a chickadee, near the rill where we'd been gathering our water. The flowing water, bubbling along the smoothed stones, carried a restful sound to my ears. There, on a large boulder, sat Gray Feather, his legs crossed underneath him and his back straight. He wore nothing to cover his chest but wore only his buckskin leggings of golden brown. His thick braid fell over his browned shoulders.

I walked over and sat next to him, though I could see he was in some sort of prayer. I crossed my legs beneath me, just like Gray Feather, and we sat in silence, except for the birds singing as they hid in the thick green of the trees. It was tranquil . . . unlike the busyness always around the wagons.

"You a strong spirit."

The sound of his voice startled me. I had never heard him speak and certainly did not expect to hear English words. His speech had a deep sound, like a demon of the dark might make but, at the same time, soothing. I looked toward his face, but his eyes were still closed and facing toward the rill.

"Me?" I asked.

"You strong. Like a bear."

I sat quietly, contemplating his words. Such a concept was strange to the ears of a seven-year-old. Just a girl.

Gray Feather bowed his head low, as if finishing a prayer, and then he looked at me.

"I watch and see your spirit. You respect creatures, like the Osage respect creatures, both wild and gentle," he said. "I see you yesterday . . . with the horse you call Erie. You not afraid of their force and you sigh gentle words to them. Words in voice they understand."

I sat quietly, taking in his words. I had never seen it before, as he described it. I just loved Erie, for he had always been a gentle horse.

"And . . . you sit here with me in the woods. Unafraid that I am Indian."

"I am not afraid," I whispered.

"I know."

"Why are you always so quiet?" I asked.

He sat thoughtfully before replying. "Ha! Not like you, always saying questions. I say only what need say."

And with that, we sat in silence, listening to the birds speak to each other, embracing nature's harmony. In spite of the early sun throwing fleeting shards of light amidst the trees, the forest was yet dimmed and cool like a stone cathedral; though I must admit, when I was seven, I had never been in a stone cathedral. We sat until we heard the movement of my family rattling the pans to break our fast. As the aroma of coffee reached my nostrils, Gray Feather and I rose together. He softly walked deeper into the woods, and I scrambled up the hill to the trail.

The men and women worked all day to get the wagon

whole and upright. Before the dinner meal, the men tightened and sealed the sideboards, then loaded the heavy items into the wagon bed and decided the bonnet, now repaired, would be stretched over the fresh-wrought frame the next morning. Grandma fussed over the items in the wagon and asked Jeremy to move the cracked spinning wheel toward the back, and to cover my ma's favorite blue chair with an oiled cloth from the chuck wagon, at least until we got the canvas secured. Grandma, her shoulders held straight and her gray hair piled high at the crown of her head, always had a mission, making sure all was right. But in the midst of her demands, she was generous with her hugs and occasional pats on the head for the little ones. My grandma was always a soft place to fall.

"Mother, tell Mariah that I will mend her spinning wheel when we're settled in Texas," said Jeremy.

"That is kind, Jeremy. I think you should tell Mariah yourself. I am certain it will make her happy, overjoyed that we can yet spin," said Grandma. "So much will need to be done when we get settled again." Grandma walked off toward the chuck wagon.

After our meal of rabbit stew, rabbits Gray Feather had captured and skinned for Ma to prepare, I gathered the tins and smiled at Gray Feather as I took his platter. He nodded. I had a sudden vision of him sending up a prayer for each rabbit as he crushed it. After handing the tins to Ma, I looked up to see Aunt Audrey walk down the trail with Edmund, but Pa, Grandpa, and Grandma were heavy in conversation and didn't notice Aunt Audrey's transgression. Ma and I walked on toward the rill with Emily trailing us. Emily, her arm still bound, sat on the same boulder where I had sat that morning and watched us clean the dinnerware.

I do not remember seeing my aunt again that evening, and I knew that Pa, and surely Grandma, would have insisted a chaperone go with Audrey if they had seen her walk away with the Frenchman. The next morning, as we were dressing in the wagon, Audrey joined us, and I heard her talking to Ma.

"Mariah, I think I am in love. Edmund. Oh, Edmund is so courtly and attentive. He feels the same for me. I am certain," said Audrey in a whispered voice, but not so quiet that I could not hear.

"Oh, Audrey, do not be so trusting. You have just met him and know nothing of him or his family. You know he needs permission from your father to court you."

"Yes. But my heart beats so fast when I'm near him. Mariah, don't tell Pa or John, but last night as the moon threw its light through the treetops, before we walked back down the trail, he kissed me. A sweet, gentle kiss."

I could see Ma look at her sister-in-law, and I could see both sympathy and surprise in Ma's face.

"You know your pa or John would never have allowed you to be alone with him. Don't you be foolish over this man who may well be married. We are leaving tomorrow morning, and you will likely never see him again, Audrey," said Ma.

Audrey's face twisted from joy to distress, her eyes dampening. I felt sad for her and her loss of such a brief happiness. Something about Edmund made me uneasy, but I was just a child. What did I know?

By nightfall the following day, our wagon was whole again and packed with our belongings. Ma was wary about reining the wagon onward after the accident, but Grandma, not being one to indulge weakness, told Ma she could do it. It was promised that Uncle Jeremy would take the reins if the weather turned bad. We would leave in the morning, early.

Audrey and Edmund exchanged many looks that evening, but I did not see them walk away together, and Grandma had a watchful eye on her daughter. I wondered if Ma had spoken to her about Aunt Audrey's feelings. Edmund was quieter than his usual dashing self. The campfire burned on a clear night, with a shining moon, and I sat close to Aunt Audrey as I saw her eyes meet Edmund's through the flames between them.

When the fur trapper rose and walked toward the trees, I heard him singing the most melancholy melody, and its meaning did not escape me.

O, Shenandoah, I love your daughter,
Way hey, you rolling river.
I'll take her 'cross yon rolling water.
Ah-ha, I'm bound away, 'cross the wide Missouri.

O, Shenandoah, I long to hear you,
Way hey, you rolling river.
Across that wide and rolling river.
Ah-ha, I'm bound away, 'cross the wide Missouri.

Audrey and I sat in rapt stillness, listening to his song, his sweet voice, while little did I know at the time the truth in his words.

"Audrey, you can write letters to Edmund. Can't you?" I whispered.

My aunt's laughter echoed back and forth through the trees, and then there were tears.

CHAPTER 5

Before the sun rose, Ma was at the chuck wagon readying a meal. Emily was still asleep, and I went to help Ma, who was holding my baby sister on her hip. I took the baby. The men began to stir and, once dressed, fed and watered the horses. The skies were clear, a good omen for our departure.

"Ma, are Mister Edmund and Gray Feather still here?" I asked.

"I don't know, dear. I have not seen them, but they are not early risers."

"Gray Feather said I was strong. Like a bear, he told me."

Ma stopped for a moment and looked at me. "Fidelia, I believe he is right. You are a strong and generous girl." Ma returned to stirring the oatmeal. "Go wake your sister and place Maureen in her cradle." Ma gently placed my baby sister into my arms. "We will be back on the trail soon this morning, so ready yourself and help Em get dressed."

Grandma joined Ma to help with breakfast, and the men gathered for their coffee. The sunrise lightened the sky toward the east as Ma spooned porridge into the men's bowls.

"Where's Audrey?" asked Grandma.

"I haven't seen her this morning," said Ma.

I stopped sudden in my tracks. Oh no. This could not be

good. There was little doubt in my mind at that moment that my aunt had run off with the Frenchman. My thoughts went to Gray Feather, for I was certain that he would not be happy about this, but as my imagination soared, Grandma marched to her wagon and then returned. The set of her face revealed the news I'd feared long before she arrived back at the chuck wagon.

"She's not in the wagon. Her satchel, her things are gone. Where do you think she has gone?" said Grandma, breathless. "Are the fur trappers still here?"

Grandma's face flinched, her hands darting about so unlike the always-confident grandmother I knew. Pa, holding a cup of coffee, was already on his feet, then Jeremy.

"Go down the hill, John. See if the trappers are here," said Grandma. Pa scampered down the slope toward the woods, his face firm with the task assigned, and he disappeared into the trees.

"Let's eat," Grandpa said firmly. "All is probably fine, so let's just wait and see."

As we took our plates and sat to eat, the air filled with the stillness of increasing angst. Few words were spoken. As Ma began collecting plates, Pa climbed up the hill, shaking his head.

"No one. I looked and looked where they'd been camping. Gone. The ashes from a small fire were cold. No one answered when I called out," said Pa. "I knew those damn scoundrels were no good. Knew from the first time I set my eyes on 'em."

"Well, sit down and eat quick, son," said Grandpa.

"But, Father. What about Audrey? We can't let her go with them," said Pa, his jaw clenched.

"You eat, son. Let me ponder."

Grandpa paced as Pa gobbled down his food and tossed his dirty tins into the chuck wagon. The quickness of his temper tightened his face and his brow, while the women and Jeremy were busy readying the wagons, but no one spoke. Except me.

"Ma . . . what about Audrey. Is she gone forever?" I asked.

"Shhh, Fidelia. I'm certain we will see her again," Ma whispered. "Let Grandpa resolve what we shall do next. I don't imagine he wants to sit here on this trail forever."

As a gust of wind rustled the treetops, Grandpa stopped pacing and called everyone over.

"We have a dilemma. A daughter who's made a reckless decision, or so it appears," said Grandpa to all of us. "I do not want to delay our journey. However, I have decided to give this one day. We shall stay here, only one more day.

"John, I am sending you out. I give you one day before we move on to the south. Tomorrow morning the wagons will be gone, but I will ask you to search and track the trappers for two days beyond that. If you cannot find Audrey, retrieve her within those three days, you are to return to the trail; ride till you join up with us. Leave her behind. Audrey will have made her own choice. I will not sacrifice the group for her. She is grown," he said. Then he looked downward and, in a softer voice, said, ". . . And foolish. I will just have to trust God that Mister Chouteau will look after her."

Silence. My pa began fidgeting and shuffled his boots in the dirt.

"That is it!" said Grandpa with conviction. "Mariah, pack John's saddlebag with provisions. John, those two have an advantage on you with their skills. Do your best. In the end, risk no lives. Not yours, not Audrey's."

I noticed he did not mention the lives of Edmund and Gray Feather. Grandpa paced again as Ma went to the chuck wagon with Pa's saddlebag.

"It's decided," said Grandpa, and he walked toward his wagon to unhitch the horses. I saw tears in Grandma's eyes. It was a sight I'd never before seen, not even when we laid my baby sister in her grave back in Indiana. Now, Grandma's youngest child, her only daughter, vanished.

Jeremy unhitched the horses, but I could tell he was angry. His jaw was clenched, and he snapped the leather as he released the horses. I did not know if he was upset because his sister may be lost to us, or if he was angry that his father did not send him for Audrey. I saw my uncle's eye twitching again. It was not the first time that I sensed Jeremy's jealously of my pa.

Pa was quickly on his way after he hugged my ma and disappeared into the trees, leading his horse behind him.

Once he was gone, sharp words between my grandmother and Ma broke the quiet. I couldn't hear every word, but I could tell that Ma had shared the conversation Audrey had with her yesterday, and Grandma was angry.

Then Ma yelled back at her mother-in-law.

"And now, because of this lovestruck girl, my husband may never return, may be killed, alone, by savages or a crazed mountain lion in the darkness of a forest foreign to him."

Grandma walked off and Ma started banging pans. I heard Maureen's cries come from our wagon.

Finally, as each of us found something to occupy ourselves in the awkwardness, I followed Ma to our wagon, where she picked up the baby and sat in her soft blue chair. She rocked the infant back and forth to calm Maureen, and dandled the baby on her knee, but it was Ma who truly needed peace. Emily nestled herself on a pallet of quilts, and I picked up my embroidery and threads and climbed out of the wagon. I found a patch of soft clover halfway down the slope, where I sat and began stitching pale pink flowers onto muslin, wishing in my mind I was still sitting in the peace of the forest with Gray Feather. Wishing that all would end well and that Aunt Audrey would return with Pa.

CHAPTER 6

Little was said that day as we all sat waiting and hoping for my pa's return. Animals were fed, food was prepared and served, but conversation was absent. The sadness was held heavy on us by a warm mist that fell all afternoon, and I took my sewing into the wagon, where Ma lit a lantern. I think we all knew we would likely be leaving the next morning without Pa. *What if he got lost in the forest? What if he could never find his way out of the forest? Hadn't my ma said there were mountain lions?*

Pa had worked long days in the fields back in Indiana. For as long as I can remember, the fields of corn flourished, but the last year had bestowed little rain. I remembered the whispers at the table about Pa having to ask Grandpa for help, to ask for money, and when Grandpa mentioned moving to Texas, Pa jumped right at the chance. But after weeks of struggle on the trail, I saw the difference in him: the set of his jaw had changed. I missed his smile and his lighthearted stories, the playfulness with Ma, Emily, and me. Now he was gone to the dark woods.

By nightfall, after our late meal, it was still quiet. There was no sign of Pa, no sign of Audrey. My sleep was fitful through the night and, though Emily tried to sleep, the ache of her arm and our whispered fears kept us awake. When dawn came, my sister had drifted into sleep and I was yet restless. As expected, after breakfast we started back on the trail as the morning sunlight filtered through the trees. The despair had not lifted; more certainly it had deepened as we led our train south, leaving Pa behind.

Expectations turned to the days ahead with my thoughts of the roads before us and my eagerness for Pa's return. I thought constantly of Pa deep in the forest, wondering if he'd found tracks, signs of the trappers. Then I wondered if Audrey would agree to come back with him, assuming he was lucky enough to find them. Audrey could be stubborn, but most of the time she was a girl with a generous heart, a heart she had given away too quickly to a Frenchman. *What if she refused to return?* Pa would be angry, maybe, too brokenhearted to return to his own pa without his sister. My thoughts fretted all day as the wagon lurched and rocked on the trail. Grandma had given Emily a tonic to help her sleep because her arm was hurting, and when the baby would wake I'd rock her or change her wrap. She would lie in my arms, looking into my eyes and chewing on Ma's coral bead necklace to ease her gums, the embroidered squirrel on her bib wet with drool. When Maureen smiled back up at me, my worries would briefly vanish, and I'd forget all about Pa and Audrey. Just for a moment.

The quiet in the wagon was broken when I heard Grandpa yelling, and I looked out the front of our wagon. There was a work wagon, reined by a young man, maybe a boy, and five rowdy-looking horsemen on the trail, heading north.

"We lost one of our wagons at the river," yelled the horseman with a gray beard, the oldest rider of the bunch, I think. "The river's current is strong, with all the rain to the north, and I counsel you wait. It's passable on an ordinary day, sir."

"Much obliged, friend. Sorry about your wagon. Anyone hurt?" yelled Grandpa, who was driving the lead wagon.

"No. Just the wagon gone. Caleb here cut the horses loose at the last minute," said the old man.

Grandpa tipped his hat as the men rode toward our wagon, and the old man nodded as he passed Ma. Because Pa was gone, Grandma was reining the chuck wagon. When I rose to put Maureen in the cradle, I saw behind us that the men were gone, but Jeremy, riding at the back of our train, fell back a bit and watched their movements.

We'd traveled a good bit of the day before we stopped at the White River and made camp at the height of the slope. The river ran full and fast, as the travelers had warned us, and I knew Grandpa was worried about the crossing. Clearly, the dilemma eased some of the earlier tensions as Grandpa and Grandma talked of our trip at the evening meal. I heard Grandma say something about Audrey being a hard-headed girl bent on making her own mistakes, and then I saw her hug Ma as she comforted her daughter-in-law with assurances that my pa would return. There was even a bit of laughter about the campfire when Uncle Jeremy told us how one day, before we arrived in Springfield, he had fallen asleep and slipped right off his horse. I wished I had seen that.

"We'll stay here in this spot a day or two," said Grandpa, "till the water recedes. And I'm hoping, in that time, John will catch up with us."

I noticed there was no mention of Audrey, and with that, I was clearly reminded that there were consequences to any decisions I might make in my own future.

Ma was nursing the baby early in the morning when I woke.

"Ma, I have to relieve myself. Can I walk down into the woods for a bit?"

"Yes, but you be careful and don't go far, only as far as I can still see or hear you. We're going nowhere today, and Grandma and I will fix the breakfast. Come on back when you hear us."

Emily began to stir as I climbed down to the ground, so I hurried into the trees, into the unknown that always enticed me.

There was only the promise of light from the east as I walked among the trees; even the birds were quiet, chirping softly as if not to wake others. The big river was to my left and I could hear the rush of water carrying its heavy bounty, such as tree limbs and, likely, bits and pieces of wagons. Looking back, I remember that morning like it was yesterday. I loved the magic within the forests.

My steps were soft and certain as I pretended to be Gray Feather, hunting the forest's spirits, at one with the poplars and firs, my footsteps muffled by the cushion of moss. I bore to my right, away from the river, in search of a rill or a glade, and it was not far before I found both.

I sat in the moss next to a creek running with clear water toward the river; I pulled my bare feet beneath me as I'd seen Gray Feather do and I found my silence. As I sat, the birdsong came, or was it that my silence allowed me to hear what I did not hear in the noise of life? Then the tree frogs chimed in to fashion a symphony. I treasured the hilled forests here in these Missouri mountains. *Would there be forests like this in Texas?*

As the sun rose and lit the cleared space by the creek, I

thought of Aunt Audrey. *Was she far gone into the woods with Edmund? Had Edmund kissed her again and was she happy?* But that sounded like a fairy tale, and my thoughts carried me to the truth of nights when she likely slept on the unforgiving ground, kept awake by the shrill of summer cicadas and waking with bug bites. With shoes not made for such, she would be climbing through mud and creeks like the one I sat before, soiling the dresses she loved so. *What would life be for her when she arrived at Edmund's home? Or did he have a home?*

I put these thoughts aside as I silenced my mind to hear the birds again, but in the distance I heard voices and the clanging of pans, and with that, I rose to return to the trail. In the forest's cover between the water and the trail, something caught my eye, sparkling as a single beam of sun found its way through the trees. It was stuck in the dirt and I brushed the soil aside to reveal an old arrowhead of chert, a sign of Indians who once roamed and defended these lands. The sparkle had come from a bit of glassy quartz revealed in the stone, exposed from the rub of years in the soil and water. A reminder that the earth was never still, always changing. I freed the relic and wanted to rinse it in the rill's water, but I knew I should go help Ma and Grandma. I slipped the treasure into my pocket and decided to wash it later. As I walked up the slope I saw a garter snake slither away, and I sent a quick prayer to God that Pa would be back today.

"Girl, there's a basin of river water by your wagon. Go wash your feet and get your shoes on," barked Grandma.

"Yes, ma'am." I pulled my shoes from the wagon and bent down to clean my feet. I took my time as I sat at the edge of the trail and dried my feet with the hem of my skirt.

I was sure that Ma would wash our soiled clothes today and I would help her or, as I do sometimes, watch the baby for her.

Breakfast was later than usual, and there were some smiles and a bit of laughter in spite of missing my pa, but Grandpa reminded us that it was Sunday, God's deemed day of rest. I told Ma about the creek where there was fresh water and took her there to clean the pans and plates. After the animals were fed and watered, and the chores done, we all gathered again near the chuck wagon and sat around the waning campfire. I imagined Grandpa might frown upon Ma and Grandma doing laundry on the Sabbath.

"We need to remember, in the midst of our journey and any hardships that we may encounter . . . and have encountered," said Grandpa with a bit of a pause, "that God will deliver us according to his plan. We must trust in Him."

He opened his Bible, but it was at that moment that baby Maureen began to cry. Emily moaned, though I was not sure if that was because of her baby sister's cries or because her arm still hurt. Grandma handed Ma her cotton shawl, which Ma tossed over her shoulder and rested the baby beneath it at her breast. Silence returned.

"From Matthew eleven," Grandpa continued. "'Come unto me, all ye that labor and are heavy laden, and I will give you rest. Take my yoke upon you, and learn of me, for I am meek and lowly in heart and ye shall find rest unto your souls. For my yoke is easy, and my burden is light.'"

He turned the pages, but then paused and looked at us.

"That 'yoke is easy, and burden is light' don't feel so true these days, does it?" Grandpa smiled. "Let's pray."

Grandpa shut his eyes, but I did not. Instead, I looked back down the trail, wishing for the sight of my father's horse.

"We trust the Lord will protect us on this journey across unknown lands. We know you have a plan for our Audrey, Lord, and we trust that she will be safe in your care. I do, God, ask that you return John to us . . ."

"Amen," I yelled before Grandpa could finish his prayer. He glared at me, but I'll always remember the smile that came after.

"And from the Psalms," he continued. "'The Lord shall preserve thy going out and thy coming in from this time forth, and even for evermore.'"

Ma crossed herself, a habit ingrained by her upbringing in an Irish Catholic family settled in Ohio. It was that Irish temper and twinkle in her eyes that had stirred Pa's notice when he first saw her, or so Pa had said over a family supper one evening back on the farm. It was funny that Pa, too, had come from Catholic roots, because the McCord family had, for years, worshiped in the Methodist congregation in Fort Wayne, or so they did before we left Indiana. Pa said that his great-grandpa had come to this country, to Pennsylvania, as an indentured servant, having descended from an Irishman killed in the first Irish Rebellion. He was a young Catholic man who made well for himself after being released from his indenture and receiving a bit of land outside Philadelphia. Grandpa said he'd married a Methodist girl, and the McCords have been Methodists ever since. But Ma, having been schooled at church, had not lost her Catholic customs and still had her coral rosary beads.

Grandma and Grandpa had five sons and one daughter, Audrey, sweet and spirited Audrey. Uncle Levi, Grandpa's oldest son, and his wife, Anna, Ma's only sister, had decided to stay in Indiana. Pa had two more older brothers who lived on their own farms in Ohio. They were uncles I rarely saw, but it was there that Uncle Levi and Pa had met Aunt Anna and Ma, sisters from a large Catholic family.

My thoughts fast returned to the present as Grandpa finished our worship. Ma pulled taut the lacing at the front of her dress and raised Maureen to her shoulder to rub the baby's back when a hearty burp broke the silence. Emily giggled.

CHAPTER 7

"Jeremy, go get your rifle. We'll go huntin' for a wild turkey or some rabbit for dinner. We should savor this reprieve as there will likely be too few in front of us," said Grandpa to his youngest son.

My uncle's face lit up like a firework. He was seldom included in the men's adventures, more often left behind to watch the farm or make sure the animals were fed. I'm certain he was asked to go with Grandpa only because my own pa was gone, and deep down I was certain Jeremy knew this too, yet his exuberance was not lessened by it.

Jeremy ran off toward Grandpa's wagon to get his rifle, and I followed Ma to our wagon, where she laid the sleeping baby on the faded quilt in the cradle. Then Emily and I followed Ma over to Grandma's wagon. Ma had carried her embroidery piece with her, and they all sat down on an old blanket to visit and stitch until the men returned. I was too antsy to sit and stitch.

I followed the trail down toward the river. The water had receded a bit and was not as brown and roaring as it had been the evening before. Then I saw the rag doll, muddied with one button eye missing, float by in front of me, too far for me to reach. The stitched mouth, appearing as a plea for help, and its one large eye looked at me, and I felt sad that I could not save it before it vanished beneath the water. I shivered a moment. All I could think of was the child it had belonged to, and I prayed within that the girl was safe.

I imagined we would cross tomorrow morning, and I pulled the found chert from my pocket and, holding tight to the stone, ran my hand back and forth in the water. I rubbed it and rinsed it again, and it shone like a jewel, its edges unevenly smoothed from nature's embrace.

I walked back up the trail, looking at the relic that lay in my hand and pondering its origins. *Had there once been bones in the ground near where I found the arrowhead? Maybe an animal for a meal. A human? Had this pierced another's heart, stolen a soul? So many years ago?* I was to learn later in life that Gray Feather's family—what was left of it, as two of his brothers had died of smallpox—was confined to the west towards Kansas as white settlers had forced the Indian tribes from their lands. This land, these hills in Missouri had belonged to the Osage and were once filled with their agonies and celebrations, the rituals of community, but now, as I walked these hills, there were only remnants like Gray Feather himself, who roamed with the white man.

When I arrived at the blanket where my family sat, Emily was restless and whining. Her young spirit had been held still too long by her bandaged arm.

"Fidelia, take your sister and play a game. Or maybe a short walk along the trail. This girl has been much confined since the fall, I'm afraid," said Ma.

I took my sister's right hand and we walked toward the chuck wagon, sitting vacant. I pulled the arrowhead from my pocket.

"Look, Em. I found this in the woods."

She reached for it, but I kept it in my own hand,

bending down so she could look at it. Her left arm was held stiff with Grandma's old shawl, but Emily gently ran her fingers over the smooth surface of the stone in my hand.

"It's called an arrowhead. Used by the Indians. For hunting, mostly," I told her. Sometimes I forgot she was only five. She ran ahead of me, looking for a new diversion, something shinier than the trinket I held, when, abruptly, the silence was pierced by a gunshot. At first it frightened me, but then I remembered that the men were hunting. All turned quiet again as Emily, startled by the noise, ran back towards me.

Supper that evening was quiet, but we were treated to a savory meal of wild turkey, Grandma's red bean dish and biscuits, and Ma made us some sweet peppermint wafers with a bit of sugar. A treat for all of us.

"I believe we'll cross that river in the morning," said Grandpa as the sun's light fell through the trees to the west and the fire's embers waned. I heard a certain wistfulness in his voice and wondered if, like myself, he preferred sitting here near the river, waiting for my pa's return.

"We'll be on our way at dawn. Get some good sleep because I want to make some distance tomorrow. Up bright and early."

I did sleep sound that night in spite of my worries for Pa. There was a breeze through the wagon and even the baby slept until Ma woke her at sunrise. Ma cooked porridge for breakfast and added some turkey on the side.

"Ma, can I have a cup of coffee?"

"No, Fidelia. You know well you are too young to be drinking coffee and fidgeting all day. Here. Just a bit," she said as she handed me her cup.

As Jeremy and Grandpa hitched the horses and oxen to

the wagons' yokes, I walked down the slope of the trail to the White River, and there stood a tall white egret in the middle of it, looking right at me with his wild black eyes. The egret, standing tall and proud, revealed that our patience and prayer had brought us to a safe crossing of the river. We took the wagons, one by one, through the water that morning as Jeremy reined our wagon through and then turned the reins back over to Ma, who was still a bit wary of the mud and water after our wagon had fallen down the embankment. We were on our way again. Away from Pa.

The days after we crossed the White River became the same, one after the other, except Uncle Jeremy told me that we were now in a land called Arkansas. On one day—I don't know which day, for they now all ran together as the same—the sky turned dark in late morning. A storm approached, and it hit with such force that we had to stop. As we stopped, the wind caught beneath the canvas on the front wagon. It was flapping high in the wind, not yet gone, and Grandpa was yelling at Jeremy to grab it, but he didn't soon enough. Like a grand white kite, it went flying about in the storm. I think it was only the pounding rains that kept it from blowing back to Missouri.

"What the hell, son! You couldn't grasp the damn cloth, keep it on the wagon? Look at our belongings, all wet. This'll keep us here another day, for certain," said Grandpa, and his scowl, I am sure, only further crushed the spirit of my uncle. But it was Grandpa's anger that truly surprised me, revealing how our journey was taxing all of us.

"William, we both tried. The wind was too strong," said Grandma, looking surprised at her husband's harsh scolding. It was not normal of my grandpa to lose his temper, and I began to foresee dreams of dread carrying us to sleep each night.

Once the storm ended, it took Uncle Jeremy and Grandpa several hours to find the canvas and retrieve it from the tree that held it. Ma made some quick repairs, and by nightfall it was done, though the repaired canvas was still damp. Grandma hung their clothing on shrubs to dry and wiped down the inside of the wagon. We'd be ready to leave in the morning. Still no sign of Pa.

Uncle Jeremy was feeding the horses early the next morning, and upon seeing him and his bowed head, I walked over and gave him the biggest hug.

"Father can never count on me, it seems. I always fail, and your Pa always shines," he said to me. He looked me in the eye and saw my distress. "But I do trust he will find Audrey and get home soon."

He kissed the top of my head.

"Thank you, Fidelia. You know, you are always the bright spot. The peacemaker," he said, and kissed my head again.

When we arrived at the fort at Harrison, I listened as Grandpa recounted our journey to the man filling our barrels with fresh corn and beans when an old hunter standing nearby spoke up.

"What fool told you to take that route? That's the old mountain trail through hell. Ya know there was a shorter way, don't ya? Well, at least, an easier one."

I watched Grandpa stand quiet, staring at this stranger as if he were an oaf. I suspected he might have been.

"Not important, sir, at this point. Done been down the trail. Naught but spilt milk just sitting on the floor. Cow done kicked it over."

"Hrmph." The man walked away shaking his head, muttering words unheard by us.

"Don't mind him," said the man filling our provisions. "But, you know, someone did send you on a mighty hard trail with those heavy wagons. Your arrival here is a testament to your perseverance and God's hand, mister."

"Amen. Was no easy journey," said Grandpa. "Any good word on the trails into Austin City, down in Texas?"

"I hear that it's pretty flat past Little Rock. Never been there myself. Some rivers to cross. Watch out for the Comanche renegades as you move through Texas, and there's a few scoundrels here and there that'd be prone to separatin' you from any valuables."

I wondered what kind of scoundrels. How do we look out for these men, or women, called scoundrels? I followed Grandpa toward the wagons as Uncle Jeremy helped the man load the barrels into our chuck wagon.

We moved on, south, from the fort, but dread began to bring long silences and short tempers. Pa should have joined us long before this day if he had kept to Pa's orders. Ma's restlessness at night only increased baby Maureen's fussiness and Emily's whining, but it was clear to me no one wanted to speak of what may have happened to Pa. By keeping our terrors unspoken, we held a flicker of hope in our hearts.

We moved forward, toward the southwest and a place called Little Rock. The landscape gradually changed, the trail becoming flatter and less rocky, and we saw a few farms in the distance. Then, as we pressed on to the south, the trail became narrower and rockier, and we found ourselves jostled about so much that we would stop early to rest our weary heads.

On one such evening as we ate our meal at camp, just as the coolness of an evening fell on us, I heard a noise in the distance, like the call of ravens. I looked up toward the sky, but instead of seeing birds, I suddenly heard the beat of hoofs and then I saw Pa riding toward us. As he neared, I could see Audrey on the horse with him, holding tight to her brother's waist from behind. Pa's face was filled with exhaustion, but his smile was wide as he saw us all stand to greet him. Audrey appeared sullen and in disarray, her hair tousled and tangled. Clearly, trudging through the forest with trappers had not bode well for her. Pa's horse came to a full stop right next to our campfire, and Ma ran to greet him, taking the reins as Pa dismounted.

"Praise the Lord! And with Audrey too," said Grandpa.

"Yes, Pa, we've been riding like hell to catch up to you. Stopped at Harrison. The man there told me you all had been through, stopped for supplies. Been gone so long . . . I knew you'd be worried about us, but I was not coming home without her, Pa."

"Where'd you find your sister?" asked Grandpa.

Pa helped Audrey dismount and she marched away to the front wagon without saying a word to any of us, her head bowed, her soiled satchel in hand. Emily and I just stared as she limped away, and I saw that one of her shoes was broken.

"I know you said to return in three days but, Father, I could not come back without her. I was determined to find them scoundrels. They were deep in the woods and it took me almost five days just to find any tracks. Two days after that I found them all near a stream, the men skinning a pile of beavers. There was blood and varmint guts everywhere. I'd heard their voices clearly from a hilltop and that lead me straight to 'em, absorbed in their work. I clearly surprised 'em."

"You look tired, son," said Grandpa.

Pa sat down with us by the campfire, and Ma handed him a plate and a cup of coffee.

"Yeah, Father. I can use some rest. But let me tell you about finding 'em. When I came upon them it came clear to me that Audrey was miserable in the midst of the skinning and the harsh conditions, not what she'd bargained on. She was stacking the beaver skins for Edmund, blood on her clothes."

Pa paused. Shook his head.

"Father, I was shocked at the sight, her skirts streaked bright red with the blood of those skinned animals, her hair tangled. I saw a certain shame in her eyes when she spied me standing there, watching her. And I could tell the two fellas were not terribly keen on her presence in the midst of the work. I made the decision right then not to press the issue of her return. I would wait, stick around and wait until they saw it for the best on their own."

"Wise, son," said Grandpa. "I take it that worked in your favor."

"Fidelia," said Ma, "take this plate of food over to Audrey in the wagon."

I looked at Ma and took the plate, then walked as fast as I could over to the other wagon. I did not want to miss the conversation, not one bit of Pa's story, at the back of the chuck wagon.

"Here, Audrey. Ma sent this over for you," I said and turned quickly, running back to my spot where my supper sat. I knew I'd get Audrey's side of this tale later.

"Her pride has been wounded and she spoke to me little

on the trip home," said Pa.

"She'll get over it. Tell me what transpired with the trappers," said Grandpa.

My ears perked up. I saw Grandma walk toward her wagon and I wondered what words would come of that reunion, but I stayed at the campfire and listened keenly.

"The Indian said trapping was no place for a woman. Said Audrey wasn't fond of skinning or traversing the rough terrain. Said woman's place was at home, in the kitchen. God bless him, 'cause I couldn't argue with that."

I watched Jeremy get up and put his plate at the wagon and then walk off toward the trees. I am certain he wished he could have gone to find his sister instead of watching, once again, his older brother be the benefactor of more adulation.

"Audrey was reluctant to leave Edmund," continued Pa, "but one evening, after the others were asleep, Edmund whispered to me that Audrey deserved better. 'Deserved the best' were his exact words. According to him, he felt Audrey should be betrothed proper and provided a fine home and servants." Pa sipped some more ale and looked over at me. "Shouldn't you be helping your ma clean up, Fidelia?"

"They're finished, Pa. Ma's gone to the wagon to nurse Maureen."

"Like I said, Father, they were surprised to see me, but I saw the elation in their eyes when I showed up. I demanded nothing, hoping I could convince the parties of doin' right."

"So, she returned willingly?" asked Grandpa.

"It took a couple more days before Audrey finally agreed to return with me. I could see she knew it best to come, to family, but her reluctance and embarrassment were evident. There was little I could do to help her save face. I can't say I was happy with the way Edmund kissed her goodbye . . . but she's back. That's what matters."

"You did well, John."

"Edmund was kind enough to share some supplies with me for our travel, and he wove together a beaver hide into a saddlebag and gave me his own bedroll. For Audrey," said Pa.

"That was good of him. I saw that fine bag on your horse. I'm not sure I would have even been able to find them, let alone be so diplomatic. Do you think we've seen the last of 'em?"

I was glad that Uncle Jeremy was not present to hear Grandpa lauding Pa again.

"Don't know, Father," said Pa.

"Well, for now, our prayers have been answered." Grandpa inhaled long on his pipe. "Off to your wagon, Fidelia. Time for bed."

"Yes, sir," I said and rose, reluctantly, to go help Ma ready for bedtime. I could hear Pa and Grandpa still talking as I walked away and could only wish I had not missed any of the story. The lantern in the second wagon glowed in the night. As I walked toward it, I wondered what else Pa would tell Grandpa, but there was little doubt in my girlish head that my aunt was heartbroken.

I pulled the arrowhead from my pocket, having snatched it twice from the laundry, and ran my fingers over the smooth relic. It made me think of all the life that had been lived in these mountains over time . . . wildlife, the human joy, and struggles over centuries. The babies born, the warriors who bled, the meals cooked, all the laughter and tears that had once echoed amidst the hills. And now Aunt Audrey, a lovelorn young woman who'd run off with a trapper, only to be sent home. Like storm clouds that gathered, spent their rain, vanished, and converged once again. My thoughts brought me to missing the company of Gray Feather. I was homesick for the farm back home in Indiana, but as I looked at the prize in my hand, I knew there would be an abundance of the unknown in front of me. I climbed into the wagon, took off my dress, and placed the shiny chert deep in my satchel.

CHAPTER 8

In the morning Audrey sat next to Grandma on the chest seat of the front wagon. I could tell from where I sat next to Ma, on the second wagon, that no one was talking, and I imagined it would be like that for many miles, though I'm certain Aunt Audrey was dead tired. She'd said few pleasantries at breakfast, but she had cleaned up and her hair had been brushed and once again twisted and pinned atop her head. I caught a brief smile when she had once looked in my direction, but it vanished as quickly as it had appeared.

Our wagons trudged forward all morning, well past the height of the sun, and then Grandpa called us to stop near a creek for a midday meal. He was clearly determined to move forward for as many miles as possible, so dinner was a quick meal and we were moving again. With the horses rested and watered, we did not stop again until the sun was near the horizon through the trees, and the cessation of movement could not have been more welcomed.

That was the last time we traveled so far and for so many hours in one day, because Grandpa almost lost one of the horses from exhaustion. Grandpa shook his head at his own foolishness, saying the creatures had pulled heavy loads for too far, without proper respite, not only for that day but for day after day since Indiana. He made an oath, mostly to himself, to be more cautious, which, he said, would clearly lengthen our journey.

Audrey helped Ma with the cooking and scarcely spoke. Once she finished eating, she excused herself and went to her wagon. Grandpa tarried after breakfast the next morning, leaving the animals to rest, and we did not leave our campsite until dinner was eaten and the wagons packed. Every one of us appreciated the reprieve before we returned to the trail, where Grandpa said we would meet up with the Southwest Trail to Texas. The weakened horse turned out to be Erie, and Grandpa tied the roan to trail the chuck wagon, ensuring he pulled no weight. He told us Little Rock was before us, where we would stop for a day and replenish our provisions. We would unknit our weary bodies in the city, he told us, and I jumped for joy at hearing his words. I must say that the expressions on the faces of my family mirrored my own joy.

With our shortened days, it was almost another week of jolts and wrenching on the trails until we arrived in Little Rock and, once there, I was eager for the peace of being still. The jostling of the trail, after days on end, had consumed my vigor and made me crave a quiet day in the woods. But the city was not where I would find such solace. I had not realized we were on the edge of town, when suddenly Grandpa directed the wagons into a place where there was a gathering of wagons, all traveling from one point to another. The town had been charitable and had constructed a water well and an outhouse for the plentiful pioneers journeying through their city, thus keeping the wagons at the outskirts of town. The sky was dimming as sunset approached, so Pa said we would stay there for the night and go into town in the morning.

"Can I go, Pa? Into the town?" I asked.

"Ask your mother. It's good with me if there's room. Jeremy and Grandma will stay here with the young'uns."

Mama said I could go, and I was up before sunrise the next morning, dressed and my hair brushed and braided before anyone in my wagon was awake. My excitement brimmed over like the bucket I filled with water and brought to the chuck wagon, where I found Grandma rustling through the pans.

"Here, Delia, take this ladle and fill the kettle up to the top. I'll start a pot of coffee. "

Grandma almost always called me Delia, except when I was in trouble and she used my full name, Fidelia Fiona McCord. The nickname made me feel special. I grabbed the kettle by the handle and filled it to the brim. I needed both hands to carry the kettle to Grandma, where I found her frying some ham over a campfire and measuring grain for porridge. She added a bit of the water to the grain and hung the pot over the fire. I saw Pa feeding the horses and oxen and ran over to him.

"Pa, I'm ready."

"Ready for what?" he asked.

"To go to town with you."

"Well, slow down. We're gonna' eat first. Your ma's not ready yet, and I've got to sort out what's in the chuck wagon and make room for supplies. Go help your ma with your sisters," said Pa and he turned toward the chuck wagon.

When all the work was done and the tins and pots cleaned, I jumped onto the seat of the chuck wagon, waiting for Pa. Ma climbed up and squeezed me over, leaving little room for another. Grandpa was on his horse and Pa jumped up to the wagon seat.

"Get in the back, Fidelia. There's room for you on those

burlap sacks," said Pa. I tumbled into the back just as the wagon lurched forward, and we were on our way to town.

My eyes grew bigger and bigger as we passed so many men, some in fancy suits and others in overalls, on their way to jobs, and ladies in fancy dresses, some carrying matching parasols, going into dress shops. There had been no dress shops near home in Indiana, and I wanted to go inside one. It was hard for me to see much as I peeked around Ma, when suddenly Pa pulled the wagon to a stop in front of a large general store. Grandpa jumped down and walked straight into the liquor store.

"Ma, can we go to one of those dress shops?"

"Fidelia, we have a long road before us and no money to spare. What would you need in one of those fancy lady shops? I stitch your dresses, for all you girls," said Ma.

Pa was hitching the horse when Grandpa walked out holding two bottles and put them in his saddlebag. Grandpa winked at me.

We all walked into the general store, Ma toting a big basket. The store was bigger than any I'd ever been in, the wooden floors dusty with flour and shelves full of goods. To my left, near the front door, I saw a glass case filled with sweets. I walked over and pressed my nose against the glass, looking at the bounty staring back at me, while Ma and Pa walked amongst the shelves, choosing what they needed, arguing over what could be done without.

"Well, girl, would you rather have a bit of that sugar behind the glass there, or would you like to see the inside of one of those dress shops?" said Grandpa, who had been standing behind me.

"Really, Grandpa?"

"Well, what do you choose?"

I didn't even blink. "The dress shop, Grandpa. Can we? Mama said no."

"Well, I don't see no harm in seeing the sights. Can't remember you girls, even your ma, ever going to a fancy dress shop. Besides, I treated myself to a bottle of rye and one for your pa."

I hugged him tight 'round his waist as my face fell into his soft belly, and he took my hand as we went to find my parents. Pa asked the vendor for a barrel of ground corn, two barrels of corn for the animals, a big sack of coffee, a bushel of white beans, four pounds of bacon, and a sack of flour and another of cornmeal, as Ma walked up with her basket filled with dried meats, cheese, a few oranges, candles, vinegar, lard, and some tobacco for the men. Pa held a large glass jar of oil for use in our lanterns. Once our tab was added up and the purchases were made, we spent some time at the street loading and rearranging the goods. We still had to stop at a mill for some oats and fodder. Pa said the horses and oxen would probably need it as we traveled through Texas.

On the way back out of town, Grandpa stopped his horse in front of one of the dress shops.

"Pull that wagon over here, son," said Grandpa.

"What are we doing?" asked Pa. He reined the horses to a halt and pulled the brake at his side.

"The ladies are visiting the dress shop," Grandpa responded.

Ma looked at me with an expression of reproof.

"I didn't ask, Ma. I promise."

"What foolishness is this? The women make their own clothes," said Pa.

"We're stopping. I can treat the girls if I wish. Here,

Mariah, get a frock, or at least some yardage, for Fidelia, you, and one for Audrey." Grandpa handed Ma some paper money and, I must say, I'll never forget the look on her face. Behind the hesitation as she took the money, there was glee in her eyes.

"You girls take your time," said Grandpa as he tied his horse to a post. "John, let's sit aside this damn dusty street and have a bit of whiskey."

When Ma opened the door of the quaint dress shop, there was a smell of new fabric, as if bright gingham and pastel piques were perfumes. A pretty woman with chestnut hair, curled and pinned elegantly with pearl clips, greeted us as if we visited her shop every week. I could not believe the beautiful things around me, an abundance of pinks, greens, blues, fabrics of all kinds on the tables and shelves built right into the walls. Ma looked over a yellow dress that the shop lady picked up and said would look lovely on me. I'd never even thought of looking lovely, as the lady had said, and the dress was fancier than any I'd had before, with pleats and a laced ruffle down the bodice to cover fastening hooks beneath, stopping just above a sashed waist, and a ruffle at the hem of the skirt.

"Here, Fidelia, go try this one. I'm going to go through these fabrics. I can sew something for me and Audrey, a little something for Emily. We can't stay in Little Rock for fittings, so the cloth is better."

The lady showed me a curtain behind which I could change my dress. The yellow dress fit a little big on me, but Ma said that was best, and the sales lady showed me a mirror where I could see it. As I looked at my reflection, I saw an image I did not recognize, except for the loose hair escaping my braids. The pale yellow of the dress, trimmed with a white collar and a wide ribbon sash, seemed to give me a light, a glow, and I twirled to watch the skirt billow. This was not the girl who loved wandering in the woods, for the reflection before me was a glimpse of the woman I aimed to be one day. A grown-up. Ma turned around and saw the smile on my face, the turn of my neck as I looked in the mirror, and she smiled at me.

"We will take the yellow dress," she said to the shop lady.

My thoughts turned fuzzy, like I was in a dream. Such a fine dress. *For me?* I saw visions of me in the sashed yellow dress, yet where would I wear it? It was too pretty for chores.

"Fidelia, go change back into your old dress," said Ma when she saw me dawdling. I glanced in the mirror at my reflection one more time before going behind the curtain to change.

When I returned to stand by Ma, the lady wrapped my new frock in brown paper she pulled from a roll, tying it with twine. Ma told the shop lady measurements for two different fabrics she'd chosen, one a deep green with white and yellow flowers and the second a pink-striped cloth with a sheen.

"Audrey will look lovely in this pink," said Ma. She told me she purchased enough of the green cloth to make a dress for herself and something for Emily. She laid notions on the table, and some threads, hooks, and ribbons.

"Oh, and one yard of these two ribbons," said Ma, handing the lady a roll of yellow and one of black satin ribbon. I had never felt so special, and from the light in Ma's eyes, I'm not sure she had either.

Just as we were about to leave, a tall, elegant woman

came into the shop, closing her parasol. She glanced at us, eyeing my ma up and down as if we were lost, but Ma said "good day" to her and opened the door with her head held high. We found the men laughing as they sat on the wooden walkway, sharing a bottle of whiskey.

"Well, well, girls," said Grandpa. "I'd expected to see you all gussied up."

Ma placed the wrapped package into my arms and turned to hug Grandpa. "I love you, Father. That's the sweetest gift in my memories. I found some lovely fabrics to sew something for both Audrey and me . . . and Fidelia has a new yellow dress. And look here, I found a sweet new bonnet for Mother."

"I cannot wait to see them. I do think this journey to Texas I've dragged us on has cost you women plenty," said Grandpa as he untied his horse. Pa put the packages inside the wagon box, then lifted me to the wagon and climbed up to the box seat, taking Ma's hand to help her up.

I had to sit on top of one of the corn barrels, my head touching the top of the canvas, as we traveled back to our camp, but it had been an exciting day, and I could not wait to tell Emily and Aunt Audrey about all I'd seen.

Chapter 9

Back at the campsite, I told Grandma about the magical town of Little Rock and showed her my new dress.

"Ma said I can wear the new dress tomorrow, but after that I have to save it for special 'casions."

"Well, I'm glad you had a good time, Delia. It's a pretty bonnet your ma brought me. Don't know where I'll wear somethin' that pretty. How about I make a pot of beans for our supper? Or, I suppose, it's a late dinner."

"Yes. Beans are good," I said. "And some cornpones?" Grandma smiled at me.

Ma was nursing the baby in our wagon, and I saw Pa take some of the hay over to the horses and oxen. Emily found me and we both walked over toward the animals and Pa.

"Whose dog is that, Pa?" I asked.

"What dog?"

"That one over there, near the well," I said, pointing.

"Don't know."

The dog was white with black spots, his hair longer than the huntin' dogs I'd seen. He was thin and dirty. I walked toward him.

"You be careful, Fidelia. He might bite," yelled Pa. Emily had stayed with Pa and was throwing hay.

I kept walking right up to that dog. He whimpered, but he was not afraid of me, so I rubbed his head and saw his tail wag. He whimpered again.

"Do you want some water?" I lowered the pail and pulled it up, scooped water into my hands, and held it to the dog. He licked it right up and seemed to want more, so I gave him more. As the dog lapped from the pail, I dipped the hem of my dress in the water pail and wiped some of the dirt from the mutt's fur. When I walked back to Pa, the dog followed me.

We enjoyed a good meal at the camp that evening, and it felt good to sit and visit, to rest from the mounting weariness of our journey. There was a new ease in everyone around me, even Audrey. The dog sat behind me through our meal, and I slipped a bit of food to him when I thought no one was looking.

"That dog's never gonna leave you," said Grandma.

"That's good, Granny. Our wagon train needs a dog, a watchdog," I said.

"We don't need no more mouths to feed," said Pa.

"I think he's a huntin' dog, Pa."

Pa frowned, so I said no more.

After we helped Ma and Grandma clean up the tins and pots, the two women repacked the chuck wagon in preparation for our continued passage. I took that opportunity to walk to Grandma's wagon with Audrey, the dog following me. Audrey lit a lantern in the wagon.

"What happened, Audrey, with Edmund?" I'd been keen to ask that question since she'd returned to us, and I settled onto a stack of quilts. "Did he kiss you again? Were you sad to leave him behind?"

Audrey stared at me. Red tendrils had fallen from her pinned hair, framing her face, and I saw a fleeting light escape from her woeful eyes. With that vision, I remembered Indiana and how my aunt's eyes would shine with sunbeams and mischief. Now she dwelled in melancholy.

"He did kiss me again. There were such tender moments, just the two of us, Fidelia. Sometimes we would walk alone, away from the Indian, Edmund taking my hand, stroking my hair in the moonlight. His kisses so sweet, not at all demanding like that boy back in Fort Wayne. I wanted to stay with him, so very much, but the trapping ways were hard. I hated the killing, the skinning of the animals . . . but that is how he made a living."

"That would have only lasted until you were back in Kansas City," I said, knowing full well that it no longer mattered.

The dog yawned, and Audrey reached down to rub his ears. The sparkle in her eyes had vanished and was replaced by gloom.

"After a few days, I knew that my leaving with him like that, into the woods, was a mistake. I missed all of you, my family, so much, yet Edmund was always a gentleman. He never took liberties, as I expected he might. Later, as I rode back with John, he told me what Edmund had said . . . that we both deserved a better start, a proper courtship. Edmund and Gray Feather knew that it would be two or three months before they returned to the city. Even if they had forsaken their work, it would have taken weeks to arrive back in civilization. Edmund had told me he had a small home in Kansas City . . . a quaint place, he said, but small. Nothing grand like I deserved, he had told me."

I saw her eyes water, and sadness fell into her shoulders.

"I told him that a small cottage was fine. Oh, Fidelia, I

knew him to be my soulmate. I knew. If only we could have met at the right place, courted, and wed proper. If I'd eventually had a cottage filled with babies to busy me through his long travels with Gray Feather. But I don't see the prospect, so far from each other. And Pa. My pa would not approve."

"I'm sorry, Audrey. Do you think Edmund felt as you did?"

"I do, Fidelia. I am certain, and that makes my sorrow even greater," she paused. "There was a quiet sadness about Edmund as I gathered my things and we prepared to leave. A look in his eyes that I shall never forget."

I took my aunt's hand and held it tight. Texas, right now, seemed so distant.

"Fidelia, your ma is looking for you," said Grandma as she stepped up into the wagon. I hugged my aunt tight and jumped out of the wagon with the dog at my heels.

I woke in the morning to find the dog curled up close to me and hoped he didn't have fleas, but he probably did. And with that thought, I scratched my ankle. Emily was fast asleep, and both Ma and Maureen rustled toward wakefulness. I grabbed the basin and scampered off toward the outhouse. At the well. I filled the basin and cleaned the dog as best I could, giving him some clean water to drink. I then filled the basin and washed myself, just in case there were any bugs, before dumping the dirty water. I filled it again from the well for Ma and Emily, and so Ma could wash the baby.

I slipped some bacon to the dog at breakfast, and I saw Pa scowl at me.

"John, it can't hurt to have a dog with us, warning of

any danger, especially when we sleep at night," said Ma.

"That's probably true," said Grandma. "Like having our own little sentry."

I knew then that my pal was going with me, and I knew it was time to give him a name. Bear. I decided to call him Bear.

CHAPTER 10

The next morning, wearing my new yellow dress, I sat next to Ma as she reined our wagon, Emily squeezed between us. Bear was following along on the trail, between Grandpa's horse up front and Pa's horse in the rear, as if he knew that was his assigned position.

"Don't you get anything on the dress, Fidelia. It is now your good dress, your Sunday dress, so there'll be no wandering about the woods or hugging that dog today," said Ma, looking at me over the top of Emily's head.

"Yes, ma'am. I'll fold it careful tonight and put it away. Don't it look pretty, though?"

"Yes, it does, Fidelia."

The baby started fussing, and I climbed in the back to pick her up.

"Put a cloth over your dress or grab one of my aprons. I don't want the baby spitting on your dress," called Ma over her shoulder. Little Maureen was learning to sit up, so we played a game of patty cake and then I gave her Ma's red beads to chew on.

We spent another fortnight in Arkansas. Grandpa was careful not to overrun the horses and the oxen, for without them we could go nowhere except on foot and he would need the animals at the farm. Audrey warmed up to her old self with the family, even forgiving Pa. She knew in her heart that Pa had only done as he'd been told.

But I remember that I would see my aunt sit quiet at times by our campfires and, catching her eye, I could still see a fleeting sadness. I, too, wondered about Edmund and Gray Feather and where they were and if they thought of me or Audrey. I daydreamed about seeing them again someday, but like Audrey, I knew it was but a daydream.

After all the days on the trail from Little Rock, and after a bit of a struggle getting the wagons across the Red River, Pa found out from a farmer that we were in Texas.

"Y'all probably been in Texas for a couple days. Straight on you'll come to Paris. Nothing like France, I hear. But if ya keep goin' toward the sun and bear south on the trail up ahead you'll be goin' to Dallas. Don't know where you're headed, but you'll run into Indian trouble if you keep heading west."

"I am much obliged, sir. We're headed for Austin City," replied Grandpa.

"Lots of settlers going there and farther south. Best of luck to ya." The farmer turned his horse down a dirt path, a path barely distinguishable from the ground surrounding it, that looked to me like it went nowhere. The hills were gone, and the forests had vanished.

"Grandpa, is this it? Where we'll live now?" I asked.

"No, Fidelia. Texas is a big place. We have a distance to go."

"Awww. I trust there will be woods near our new home."

We stopped that night on a flat plain. Flat as far as one could see. The sun set to our west and the whole sky turned shades of pinks and oranges, a sky like none I'd seen before.

The journey to Dallas took forever, or so it seemed, and once we camped there, Pa and Grandpa spent the evening in a saloon while the rest of us sat around the campfire at the edge of town. Jeremy stayed with us, but he was none too happy about it. He paced about, mumbling that he was nineteen and old enough to go to the saloon with the menfolk.

"It's about time Father knows I am a man," he said. "I always get left behind."

"Son, he knows that, and that is why he left you here to protect us. He relies on you," said Grandma. "I'm sure they went for some whiskey, but they're also hunting particulars on Austin City, about the trail, about dangers that might befall us."

Grandma handed her youngest son a tin of ale and smiled at him. Back in Indiana, Ma had told me that Audrey and Jeremy had come long after Grandma thought her family was finished, giving her two toddlers to chase along with all the men she mothered. Pa always said his baby brother and sister were pampered, but I never saw it that way.

We sat by the campfire, talking of the journey behind us and laughing until it was late. I saw Uncle Jeremy help Ma put out the campfire and take the mugs to the well to wash. Bear looked toward Ma and Jeremy, then followed me to the wagon and snuggled up next to me and Emily on a pile of quilts inside. I wondered what kind of watchdog he was, sleeping here on the soft quilt.

Grandpa had told us we could sleep as late as we wanted. I heard baby Maureen wake Ma early, but Emily and I rolled over and went back to sleep. We all stayed at the campsite while Ma and Pa went to the market for provisions and returned with the chuck wagon loaded. I was bored all day. There were no woods where I could roam, so I did a bit of embroidery and then watched Ma stitch the dress she was making for Aunt Audrey. It was going to be so pretty with its soft drape and the white collar that Ma was stitching to add at the neckline. I could not wait to see Audrey wear it, with her red hair falling onto the pink stripes.

In the afternoon, I wandered over to Grandma's wagon and visited with Aunt Audrey. I found her sitting under a tree on a blanket , reading a book of poetry. Audrey always liked to read but had only two books of her own. She held *The Hours of Idleness*, the poetry of Lord Byron, a book she was gifted by a teacher when she was in school. I envied her love of reading, for I found it a struggle to sit still long enough to read the words Ma taught in my readers. With our travels, Emily and I had been relieved of our studies, but it surprised me that at times I would yearn for Ma's readings and lessons.

Bear and I sat next to Audrey, careful not to disturb her reading, and I leaned back and watched the clouds. I could not believe that I was antsy to return to the trail, to be on our way again. Surely one day we would stop, and we would live in a house again.

After a day spent outside of the town of Dallas, a day of rest, more for the horses than for us, we were again on our way. Grandpa said it would be nearly ten more days to Austin City, but we would have to cross the Brazos near a place he called Waco. Though anything could happen in ten days, I began to feel an excitement for the end of our travel, to see the place that would be home for us.

The Brazos River was low as the heat of a Texas summer converged upon us, so, except for the rocky passage on the river bed, we had no trouble with the river crossing. I saw trees all about us, but there were no tall poplars and pines like those of home or the trails we had crossed. On the ninth day after leaving Dallas, Grandpa said we had arrived. Audrey and I jumped for joy, holding hands and dancing around. Emily joined in with us just for the pure joy of it.

"We're camping here for now," said Grandpa. "John and I will ride into the city in the morning to get a feel for where we are and to look for a cabin and some farmland. Let's set up camp. Don't know how long we'll be here."

In the morning Pa felt poorly, and Grandpa decided to go into the city without him. Pa fed the horses and then went into our wagon and laid down on the quilts where Emily and I slept at night. Grandpa rode away toward Austin City to seek leads on farms for contract.

Late in the afternoon Grandpa returned with some leads on land. Pa still lay in our wagon, asleep, and Grandma said he was fevered. In the morning, Grandpa went alone to find one of the contacts he had been given at the Land Office, a man called Franklin Brown. When Grandpa returned, Grandma told him that Pa was in a terrible way as the fever had hold of him, and Ma soothed Pa with cool, wet rags.

"I think I've found us a place, and from what I see of John's condition, the sooner we get settled, the better," Grandpa said. "It's a cabin near a pond fed by the springs, a bit of farm land. Enough for now. Jeremy, get the oxen hitched up and I'll get the horses. Let's get settled and get John in a proper bed."

I was worried because I could see that Grandpa was distraught. Surely Pa would be well again. He was strong. I helped Ma pack the chuck wagon, and we were on our way, jostled again on a stony trail. I could not wait for the jostling to end.

The pond was big with abundant trees around it. The cabin appeared small, but big enough with two bedrooms and a large loft upstairs, a room that Uncle Jeremy would later finish into a hallway and two bedrooms. Inside, the rustic home surprised me, for the floors were fine wood with tall windows dressed in muslin and tied-back drapery that would provide warmth in winter. The stairway was finely finished with a hint of a curve at the bottom, widening the steps. On the inside, the old farmhouse appeared a fine home one would expect in a big city. I could not help but wonder who had lived here before.

There were a few pieces of furniture and bedding, and Grandma went right to work pulling the linens from the wagon and told Jeremy to pound out the feather-filled bedding outside, then place them on the pallets and frames in the bedrooms.

Everyone was busy, carrying supplies to the barn and the house; Grandpa shouted orders to us all. Ma found the well and went straight to tending Pa. Grandma decided to feed us that evening from the chuck wagon and a campfire . . . she said she'd get the kitchen cleaned and the stove working the next day. We all sat for supper at the big table in the kitchen, like a family, but Pa was absent.

As happy as we were to be home, settled again, an unspoken fear had settled over us all. Pa was ill, and we were in an uncharted land. Grandpa said little at the supper table, only grace.

CHAPTER 11

Within the week, both Audrey and Jeremy fell to their beds with the fever, like my pa. The heaviness of worry filled the house, and Pa was yet gravely ill. Grandpa cared for the animals, turned a field to plant a fall crop to pay the rent, and he made repairs to the fences and the barn, while Ma and Grandma worked day and night comforting the ill. Grandpa was happy to find an old, rusted plow in the cowshed to use until he could purchase a proper one.

Ma told Emily and me to stay away from the sickness, and it was my job to care for baby Maureen, except when Ma was nursing. At times, when Ma needed a brief respite or a quick nap, we would go sit amongst the trees near the pond, where Emily and I would play and run with Bear.

I helped Grandma in the kitchen when the baby was sleeping, learning to do a bit of the cleaning and cutting wild onions or kneading the bread. Grandpa had no help with the work, but he rode into town one morning for some provisions. The cupboards were bare, and he returned with sacks of beans and potatoes and some cornmeal. Two of the chickens had survived the trip from Indiana, but we would need more, said Grandma, and a dairy cow. Grandpa found a nearby farmer willing to trade a cow for one of our oxen and he sold us four hens too. Grandpa showed me how to milk the cow, and it became my first chore of the day for years to come, meaning I needed to rise before the sun. It was my favorite chore, for I found it was a quiet time, to myself, alone, delivered by the solitude of dawn.

I wanted so much to visit with Aunt Audrey, to see Pa, but I did as Ma told me, in addition to keeping an eye on Maureen and Emily. For now, Grandma and I could put a bit of food on the table. Too often I saw my ma in tears when she came from Pa's bed. For now, Grandma had the patients in beds downstairs, so the rest of us shared the sleeping pallets in the loft. Pa's fever would not abate, and Ma feared losing him. I remembered baby Hester's funeral, back in Indiana, and could not bear to see my own pa go there, to that dark place.

Grandma was stoic in her care of her children, and I stayed nearby, keeping basins and linens ready for her use. In addition to helping Grandma in the kitchen, I even learned how to churn the butter from the cow's milk. It was hard work for a seven-year-old's skinny arms, but I got stronger each day, and in the evenings, after supper, I would walk Bear along the pond. I cried. Cried for the fate my uncle, my Pa, or my Aunt Audrey might meet. I cried for the weariness of our family.

On one evening, a warm dusk surrounded me. The Texas sward framed the pond where willows and cottonwoods stood tall at the north side. The scorching west sun warmed the water, and with the sun now only an orange half-orb in the distant west, the fireflies flitted above the rested water, a chipping sparrow sang out, and the frogs began croaking. I soaked in the serenity and my surroundings, and it was there that Emily found me by the tree.

"Sissy, you are sad?" She hugged me. Grandma had removed the cloth holding Emily's injured arm, and though some stiffness was obvious, my sister seemed her old self. Her hug gave me comfort. Emily was a giggler, and I loved her constant optimism.

"Let's run by the pond with Bear and then go help Grandma in the kitchen," I said.

I began running with Emily, Bear barking and chasing the both of us, only stopping when we ran out of breath.

"I need to get the baby up and clean her before Mama nurses again. Let's go," I said.

The short run in summer's heat cleared my head and dried my eyes, and Emily and I went to the house to help Grandma. Maureen was fussing and, before Ma came to nurse, I had changed the baby's gown and nap and wiped clean her neck that was wet with drool and spit. Grandma let me mix the cornbread, and we ate bacon and beans with the pones that evening.

After supper, as Grandma filled a bowl with well water and gathered cloths for Jeremy and Audrey, Ma came with good news.

"His fever has broken. Praise the Lord. Praise. Praise. John's fever is gone. Praise!" She was so joyful she was almost dancing.

"Oh, God, thank you," said Grandma. "Now we must keep praying for Audrey and Jeremiah. Mariah, go tell Grandpa the good news." Grandma walked into the bedroom to comfort her youngest son and her only daughter.

The following day, Pa was out of bed and eating with us at the table again. Though he was still weak, he wanted to head to the field to work beside his father.

"You will not," said Grandma, her voice firm. "Before you end up back in that bed again, you will rest and eat well for at least two days. Then you can ease back to work."

Grandma was not one for lazing about, but she knew how easily one could relapse into illness. Pa was confined, so I sat with him part of the day. I told him how we had prayed for him, and for Jeremy and Audrey, and how Grandpa had got more chickens that were laying lots of eggs in spite of the terrible heat.

Grandpa said the horses were suffering from the heat in the barn and he worked late into evenings, digging holes for the fence posts and expanding the corral for the horses and the remaining ox. My sweet grandpa looked dead to this world at the end of each day. It was clear to me that carrying all the work alone did not bode well on his being. All I could do was hug him whenever I walked past.

It was the next day that my beautiful aunt died.

CHAPTER 12

For all the distance from Indiana, for all the long days to get to Texas, not one day did I find as sorrowful as this one. Little did we know what was to come. The rooms in our new home felt like a charnel house, and we were all grief-struck. First Hester last winter, now Audrey. The weeping in the house would not stop as we prepared for a funeral.

Grandpa had visited Mister Brown about burial grounds. The land we lived on was not our property and we had no permission to bury family there. Our landlord helped Grandpa arrange for a plot in a small cemetery in Williamson County, just northeast of our home. We had no minister.

It was on that day that my uncle's fever broke, and he rose from his sickbed, only to be sent back to bed by Grandma. She prepared a broth and took it to him.

The words were unsaid, but I knew that deep in my ma's heart she was grateful to God that Pa was spared, yet, to assuage remorse for such thoughts, she had sewn day and night to finish the pink-striped dress she had started for her sister-in-law. She tatted threads to add a strip of lace to the collar's edges and stitched each fastener onto the bodice as if her sister-in-law were to attend a ball. She cuffed each sleeve with a black satin ribbon to tie and to match the black band covering the bodice fasteners. As Ma sewed, Grandma prepared her daughter's body for the grave. Grandma tried to hold a brave face, but I saw her reddened and damp eyes.

All this way we'd come. All this way to lose the able and vibrant Audrey. After breakfast, Grandpa headed straight to the workshop in the barn, where, without saying one word, he nailed and formed a coffin for his youngest child. I could not believe how beautiful, even in death, my sweet aunt looked in that box, in the sheen of her crisp new dress and her red locks laying against her white collar and her ashen visage. Yet as lovely as she appeared within the bounds of a coffin, the grip of death had stolen the rose of her cheeks, her glee. As I looked at her there, I suddenly had a thought and yelled "Wait" before the coffin was nailed shut.

I ran up the stairs in search of Audrey's satchels and dug through them for her Lord Byron book, then ran back to the barn.

"Here. She must have this" And, though I wanted to place the book in her hand, I only placed it nearby, for I did not want to feel the coldness of her skin. I remembered her as warm and filled with dreams and zest that was often reckless.

On the morning of Audrey's funeral, there was a knock at the door. It was Ethel Brown, our landlord's wife, with a basket of food.

"I have come to say that my husband has already dug your daughter's grave," she said. "You need not worry about it being done. It's done. I pray God be with you, for your losses are unimaginable. My husband has arranged for our pastor to attend this afternoon, and you are all welcome to our church group for worship on any Sabbath."

She reached out first to my grandmother and hugged her, then my ma. She turned to leave. When she opened the door, I could see, behind her, Grandpa and Pa placing the coffin into our wagon.

"No," said Grandma. "You stay with us for a bite. Let me pour you some coffee. We are grateful for your thoughtfulness, Ethel. Please, sit here."

Ma fried up some eggs, and we had jam with fresh-made biscuits. Amidst the sadness there was a gratitude for having a new friend, for my family had never felt so alone.

After our dinner, we gathered once again at a cemetery, where I saw the pile of dirt next to another pit, though larger than the one for my sister Hester. Grandpa, Pa, and Mister Brown lifted the coffin from the wagon and, with ropes beneath, lowered my aunt into the earth. It was the first day of September, and a rare soft rain cooled the air as we said our goodbyes to Audrey. The pastor, a young man, opened his Bible and read verse, but my thoughts were elsewhere. My first thought was that I was too young to be at another funeral, but I felt Emily holding tight to my hand and held that this was new to her.

Then my mind traveled back in time. I could not stop thinking about Edmund. Gray Feather and Edmund did not know that dear Audrey was gone to heaven. If only we had let her go when she'd escaped for a new life. If only she had gone to Kansas City, if she and the love of her life had run off together, she would still be alive. She would be happy. She would be in love and one day she would have been a mother. Her cheeks rosy, her spirit shining. We had changed her path, different than the one she had chosen, and I wept, right there in front of everyone, standing next to my ma. My tears kept coming, and Ma reached for me and pulled me close to her and I let my tears flow into her skirt.

I can tell you now, as I tell you these stories, that this was a moment that has never left me. The life lessons carried forward with me are from, and will always be from, my beloved Aunt Audrey, lessons of consequences and loss. Of paths chosen and those forsaken, the price to be paid.

For the next few days, I was filled with a weight of grief that I had never experienced before. A heaviness that sat inside my chest like a boulder. My thoughts went, unwilling, to the graveyard. My tears would fall unexpectedly. *Would the creatures of the soil visit my aunt? Would the worms tunnel their way into Audrey's courageous heart?* But the work of the farm persisted, and I found myself back at my chores, spurting warm milk from our cow each morning as the sun rose. The busyness helped to regain my focus, helped me find my smile again when Maureen started crawling about the cabin and when Bear licked my face. Grandpa seemed to wander about the farm, almost aimlessly. I could see him deep in thought, but most of all, I saw the toll of sadness that ravaged his soul.

We joined the Browns at the pastor's home on the following Sunday and began to make friends. Ma began sewing again and worked on putting lessons together for my schooling, and Emily was now old enough to start learning her letters. I thought of the Lord Byron poetry book and wished we had it, but I knew Audrey needed it and loved it more than I ever would, or so I had thought at the time.

The following Sunday morning there was a celebration for Maureen's baptism. She was dressed in the white embroidered dress Ma had kept from earlier baptisms, and when Pastor Wieland sprinkled holy water onto Maureen's head, she squealed right in the midst of the ceremony. I did not remember being baptized, but Ma had told me that I was baptized back at the church in Indiana, as well as Emily and Hester. As everyone bowed their heads in a prayer of blessing, I sat wondering what made the water holy. Looked like creek water to me.

Pa and Grandpa planted fields of winter squash and onions and prayed for rain. When things started to seem normal again, the first of the horses died. After our grueling journey to Texas, the daily work in the fields, pulling the plow, coupled with the harsh sun and sweltering temperatures, they could endure no more. They weakened as they refused water, what they needed the most. One by one they dropped, and by the end of September, we had lost all but one horse. Grandpa looked defeated. Pa, angry.

Chapter 13

The weather began to cool as October waned, and the fall crops thrived. The months before winter were full of hard work in harvesting the last of our crops, but fruitful enough to cover the rent and buy two horses. Pa had not been himself since he was sick, but I didn't know if it was his illness followed by back-breaking work or if it was the losses and struggles we had suffered that broke him. He seldom smiled as I remembered he had back in Indiana, and his brooding silence was peppered with harsh words. I must confess that I, too, felt a homesickness for the Indiana farm and family we'd left behind, a home now but a vision in my head made sweeter by its distance. The growing tension between Pa and my ma made me wary, but I settled myself into Grandma and Grandpa's persistence and hopes that held the family together. On occasion I would find Ma sitting alone on the edge of her bed, her head in her hands as if she'd been crying, but she would smile upon seeing me, pretending that all was well. Grandma worked long days in the kitchen and the vegetable garden, and Grandpa was the dreamer, his heart always filled with optimism.

Grandma struggled writing the letters home to Indiana to tell the family of Audrey's fate and the details of our journey. Unspoken regret filled our home, a weight I often felt swallow me, and I'd worry about my own future. Grandpa would often go to Brushy Creek or to the Colorado

River, a pastime where he found his peace fishing for catfish and bass, and Grandma and Ma were always grateful for a fresh catch. It lifted my spirits to go with him as I'd carry my basket of bait and my willow fishing pole that Uncle Jeremy had made. Growing up younger than his brothers, my uncle had found the workbench a solace to his loneliness. He could saw and sand and craft just about anything one asked for.

The serenity Grandpa found standing in the quiet of a morning by the water, waiting, would often carry my mind to the days when I'd wandered by a rill in the Ozark woods. Those memories coupled with the patience of waiting for a bite on my line always renewed my joy, sent me home a new girl ready for the next day. Grandpa would sometimes sit with me by the pond and talk about his sprite of a daughter, Audrey. The tales he shared were always happy ones. One morning, he told me of a summer day in Indiana, when my aunt was only six and learned to ride her brother Levi's favorite stallion at his farm, how her red hair flew in the wind as she rode, how she laughed, and how the laughter rang across the meadows. Told me how the young men at the neighboring farms would come courting his only daughter, but they never stayed long, for Audrey had exacting standards. I knew the pond and the creek were Grandpa's preferred places where silent prayers passed through the morning dew to God and back, and I savored sharing those sacred moments. I loved being near Grandpa, for I felt in many ways that I'd lost my own pa.

The last of the winter crops were harvested in late November, just before the first freeze. The skies turned gloomy, the large willows and hackberries danced in the windstorms that blew through, and Ma moved our classes to the dining table. Pa and Grandpa had scouted the area for some homestead land, and Pa found some he liked near a creek called Cypress. He went into the city to see about a homestead, but the land he found had been spoken for by another.

The year of undoing had taken my pa to a darker place, a place that had shut out the rest of us. He'd lost a baby daughter, and then his young sister. He'd left a thriving farm in Indiana for a land that had killed the horses and showed fragile promise for crops. He spoke little, and when he did, his words were hard and filled with regret. He'd been lucky to survive the fever, but I'd seen the changes come even earlier. When Edmund showed up, when the wagon fell, the brutal days where the horses and oxen could together take only one wagon at a time up a Missouri hill, and Pa would walk the animals back down the steep hill for another wagon. I watched the joy he had once found in farming and in his family drain out of him. The smiles disappeared, his hugs and playful gestures to woo Ma faded away day by day, and with that I saw my mother draw within herself.

Pa seldom went to church with us. I loved the ritual and the dinners and the new friends I met at the home of the pastor just beyond the cemetery. The pastor, Jacob Wieland, was a young man who had not been in Austin long but was eager to build a church and community. He laughed easily, and I liked that about him.

I remember one cold December day when the pastor came in a small wagon to our home. The Christmas rituals were nearing, and he had a small fir tree he said was from the east pines and told us it was a German custom to decorate this to celebrate the birth of Jesus.

"I think your girls will enjoy the custom, Missus McCord. We string some popcorn and put it on the tree and some people put candles upon the boughs," said the pastor to Ma as he carried the tree into the house and set it in a pail. "It will need a bit of water to keep it fresh."

"We'll be having no tree in our house, pastor," said Pa, who was sitting at the table. "God clearly meant for the trees to grow outside and 'tis not our custom."

"But, John," said Grandma, "he's merely trying to bring us some celebration with the Lord's day. It will be good for us."

"No," said Pa and he walked out of the room.

The pastor took the tree out of the house, and he and Grandma found a lovely spot near the barn to place it. Grandma brought a bit of water from the well for the pail, and they set the tree straight with some stones.

"Let the children decorate it as they wish," said the pastor. "I am sorry if I caused any trouble here, but the children will have fun with it. Bless you and your family, and I will see you on the Sabbath."

"You will," said Grandma as Emily and I touched the soft boughs of the tree. Pastor Wieland left in his wagon.

It was not long after that day, in the middle of December before the holy days and the new year, when Maureen fell ill with the fever. The look on Ma's face was more than I could bear, and Pa became even more distant. Our landlord, Mister Brown, was kind enough to send a doctor to our home, but the doctor said there was little we could do but keep her comfortable, and he suggested we pray the fever would break. He said it looked like scarlatina, an illness prevalent among the children.

"Do you think that is what killed my sister-in-law last

summer?" Ma asked the doctor with a trembling in her voice that I had not heard before.

"It is possible, ma'am. It is one of the fevers that we can do little for but wait it out and pray that it breaks. A wet rag, especially about the face, forehead, will give some comfort."

He gave us a tonic to aid sleep and advised Ma to enhance Maureen's nursing with some well water, but Ma told him the child was nursing poorly.

When Pastor Wieland came to visit one morning, Pa walked out the door and headed to the barn. The pastor sat for one whole morning with Ma as she tended Maureen. The young pastor was a kind and persistent man, and worry riddled his face. He had not forgotten our misfortunes from the past summer.

In a week, Maureen was gone like the others. Again, one more burial, one more grave. I clung to Emily. Emily clung to me.

CHAPTER 14

Pa dug the grave for Maureen in the morning, near Audrey's grave, but he refused to stand with the preacher and the family at the service in the afternoon. He stayed home.

"John, it's your daughter. Your baby daughter," Grandma had said. "At least do it for Mariah, for your own wife."

"I'll listen to no more words from that pastor," Pa said. "And God! Where is He? He vanished from my life the day I left Indiana. You can go and praise that Lord you believe in, the one who has taken so much from me, from us. I have work to do in the barn."

With those words, Pa grabbed his coat and walked out, slamming the door behind him. In spite of Pa's isolation from all of us, his words tugged at my heart. They were sad words that disheartened me. I, too, did not want to stand before another grave in the cold, only to send away another whom I loved.

I kept thinking of Grandma's words, oft repeated by Ma and by Grandpa . . . how my sisters, my aunt, had gone to heaven. Maybe Pa was right. *Where was this place called heaven? Who would take these sweet girls away from those who loved them so much, beloved family who'd done no harm to anyone? Take them from those who needed them? God would do that? Were they all deceiving me, trying to soothe my misery with fairy tales? Or were they only trying to mollify their own grief?*

But I would go today, to the graveyard, and hold my ma's hand because I knew she would need the comfort. All of us needed mercy. I knew that I would keep searching for it because Father's despair was not a place I wanted to go.

"Delia!" I head Grandma calling and ran toward the sound of her voice.

"Here," She placed a damp shirt in my hand. It was the day after we'd buried Maureen. "Help me hang this laundry to dry. Before those clouds over there drop rain."

She pinned Emily's worn pink dress, a dress that was my own before it was hers, to the line. I reached for pins in her basket to hang the shirt and passed a chemise into Grandma's hands. The darkening sky promised rain, but it was far enough that the breeze and the warmth of the January sun might first dry the laundry.

The next morning, I saw Jeremy turning an empty field so that it would be ready for the spring planting. I gathered the hen's eggs for Ma and saw Pa and Grandpa in the barn.

"Father, we can't afford another summer like the one last year. What'll we do if the cursed heat kills our crops, our animals? What does this season, or the next year's, hold, Father? What?"

Grandpa placed his hand on Pa's shoulder, a loving gesture my pa rejected as he stepped back.

"Son, find yourself some land to your liking. The city is growing and there will be markets. I'll help you build a cabin. Texas is giving land away to married men like you, hundreds of acres. Take it," said Grandpa, searching for some glimmer of faith in his son.

"And, Father, just how do you suggest I plow and plant and harvest a hundred acres on my own? With no sons to help in the fields. Watching livestock, as if I had any, die before my eyes. Parched crops that bring no profit. Tell me, Father," said Pa, his voice filled with scorn.

I did not like the sound of anger I heard in my pa's voice, but it was his remark about having no sons that had caught my breath. He still had two daughters. I sat on the nearest hay bale and continued to eavesdrop.

"I have profited, son. Moreover, we no longer shovel the snow from our hearth in winter as we did up north. Do we?"

"I would welcome the snow. It waters the roots, does it not?" Pa's words rang hollow and bitter.

"Success comes with time, with effort, and especially with family and friendships. I don't know how to help you help yourself. We came here for opportunities, and you need to grasp those prospects, son."

I imagined Pa had glared at his father, for I did not hear him answer Grandpa. My pa walked right past me as if I wasn't there and on toward the horse stalls.

On another morning, after breakfast, Grandpa went so far as to suggest cattle driving to his son, handing him a poster from someone looking to hire drivers for a ranch in Lampasas, but my pa had no inclination toward herding cattle.

"Son, they're paying thirty dollars a month."

Pa looked at the paper then back at his father. "You trying to get rid of me, Pa? Says here I gotta travel to Montana and dodge hostile Injuns. What the hell!"

Pa crumpled the paper in his hand and glared at my grandpa. Farming is what my pa wanted and what he knew, and every day I saw his growing discontent as he grappled with this new life in Texas.

After our year of such loss, my family hunkered down, burying themselves in the work and the routines of what we called ordinary days, where the sun rose and set with predictable regularity. We would go to bed each night with fatigue so heavy that we thought of nothing, memories and dreams misplaced. Even Emily and I, girls with wandering minds and playful spirits, found our chores a comfort in the offering of the promise of more joyful tomorrows.

With the money my ma and grandma had earned from some mending and dressmaking, Grandma purchased more chickens and began selling eggs and cakes at the market in Georgetown or in Austin on market days. Often, leaving Emily at home with Ma, I would help my grandmother sell the goods from the back of our wagon. When we traveled to market in Austin City, I would see servants and Negro slaves sent to buy goods for the fancy ladies who lived in big houses, and the laughter and smiles of these servants did not escape my notice. In spite of their worn clothing and bare feet, their smiles revealed the joy of their market trips, time filled with fresh air and a reprieve from their house chores and the ties that bound them. The young women would giggle and visit with each other, and the older slaves wore a sense of ease on their faces, making me wonder what my life would be like should I have been such a servant, indentured or enslaved.

Sometimes a slave would have a child on her hip. Sometimes the child was clearly not her own but the child of her mistress. I thought of how these mothers and nannies had to work dawn to dusk in the fields or in large houses. Every day. My thoughts struggled with the chance of how some of us were free and others were not.

Oddly, that very topic arose at our midday meal on the day after I'd had my musings of the life of a slave.

"The godforsaken president can't decide if this state will allow slavery or not. The vote to annex the republic as a state is done. Let us be. Now they've signed a treaty with Mexico. Glad I didn't sign up to fight in that war, to fight for nothing," said Pa at the dinner table.

"Son, they've always had slaves here in Texas, ever since they started farming the land, so I imagine nothing will change. It's a shame so many had to die fighting over that border to the south, but President Polk has gained our nation much territory through the treaty he signed to end that war.

"And to the matter of slavery," Grandpa continued, "it is an abominable institution, yet in a land that grows cotton, with its hard labor and without the grand plantations of the deep south, even I would relish the help. But I would want to bind no human being to a life not their own. I fear this dissension will continue to split us, son." Grandpa paused and asked Grandma for more coffee. "Thanks to God, at least, the war is finished, but I think the Free Soil party will throw this election to the wind. And that treaty Polk just signed with Mexico . . . got the Whigs faltering."

"Well, it's not my concern, Father. Right here, on this land, it is I who am the indentured labor."

With those words said, Pa rose and left the room. Grandpa shook his head and looked at us with despair etched deep in his face.

I celebrated my eighth birthday in January with Grandma's spice cake. I felt much older than my age after undergoing the anguish of the past year. I held an eerie sense of maturity inside, unfamiliar, as if the soul of my Aunt Audrey had dwelt within me and I could see the world through an older soul, through her woeful eyes. Life held so much chance in spite of our hard work, our plans. So much of the unknown in life carried our days down paths that could alter at a glance. And it was clear to me that my having such awareness was itself wisdom beyond my young years.

Yet, like Grandpa, I was hopeful for the future.

CHAPTER 15

An early spring bestowed rains for the new year, and brilliant wildflowers, some strange and nameless to me, sprung from the earth, offering promise. Promise had been scarce for our family and could not be more welcome.

As March approached, Pa and Grandpa were busy planting cotton in the two large fields, potatoes and onions in the others. A good early spring rain or an early Saturday morning would draw Grandpa to the pond or the Colorado River. Pa wanted no part of sitting quiet by the water, and at times he grumbled about the work left to him and Jeremy.

As March neared its end, there was a visitor, a most unexpected guest. I was outside with Emily and Bear when I saw the man in a uniform, a soldier, a long rifle slung at his shoulder, walking up the path to our home. Across his blue jacket was a red and white band crisscrossed down to a saber at this hip, his figure held straight with a confident gait. He led a fine black horse behind him. I was unsure if I should run to greet the stranger or go to the fields and tell Grandpa. As Emily ran 'round a tree, playing behind me and taunting the dog, I stood still, spellbound, and watched as the man approached.

As he neared, all of my apprehension vanished, and I ran to greet him, throwing my arms about his waist and nearly knocking him over.

"Whoa! That is a greeting," said Edmund as he slipped his saber into a leather holster on his horse saddle. "Delia, isn't it? *Bonjour, la petite.*"

"Yes," I answered, enchanted that he remembered my Grandmother's nickname for me. "Why are you here? Are you a soldier now? Where is Gray Feather?"

"*Mon Dieu*, so many questions." He smiled a large, joyful smile. He looked different without his beard, even more handsome than I remembered.

"I've come to speak with your grandfather about a serious matter. And to visit with your family, and of most importance, with Audrey. Is she well?"

Emily had joined us, and Edmund picked her up. I was not going to be the one to tell him of Audrey. No. That is not news I could bear to tell him, and I pretended that I had not heard his question. Together, the three of us walked toward the house. Though I was jubilant on the outside, a sadness gathered deep in my chest for the news my friend would soon hear.

"I have been fighting for the states, the United States, in Mexico and in Texas near the rivers to the south. Oh, such grand and large lands there. And Gray Feather. The last I saw him, he was leaving for Kansas to see his family."

He tied his horse to the post and knocked at the door of our house.

"No, Edmund. Mister Edmund." I called him by his given name as I knew well that I could not properly pronounce his last name. "We can just go in."

I opened the door and entered, pulling him inside. Ma and Grandma looked up to see us, and I could tell that, at first, they did not recognize him, being shaven and in uniform. Then Ma smiled in greeting, and Grandma glared.

"Madame McCord," he said, looking straight at Grandma. "I come wishing no malice. I confess I was wrong to let your Audrey come with us when we were in the mountains. I am here with good intentions, I assure you."

"Sit down, Edmund," said Ma. "Put your things down and sit at the table. I'll get you a drink, but I don't expect my John will be too happy to see you here."

"You've been at the war?" asked Grandma, softening a bit.

"Yes, ma'am. Joined up when I got home last year, last summer. Been fighting the Mexican army since then, south of the Rio Grande mostly, under General Taylor."

"Delia, go get your Grandpa and tell him to come in," said Grandma. "Just Grandpa." Then she gave me a stern look that I understood.

Grandpa did not shake Edmund's hand when he came into the house, but he eyed the visitor up and down and glanced at the weapon and knapsack leaning in the corner. We all sat at the table, except Pa and Jeremy, who were out in the field plowing. Edmund was immersed in sharing his tales of fighting with the army, describing the harshness of the land near the Rio Grande.

"That's a nice rifle you got leaning against the wall over there. A Spencer?" asked Grandpa.

"Yes, sir. I was in the artillery and the general issued it to me. That *belle* . . . uh . . . beautiful piece saved my life more than a few times. I am a captain in the army for the states, heading home to Missouri now, where the Army will sign my release. Or maybe I shall stay here in Texas, depending on your answer to my question and how Audrey feels. It is my desire to stay."

At the mention of Audrey's name, a brutal silence

settled at the table. Such a wretched quiet that I could hear the leaves rustling in the breeze outside. A breeze that carried, so swiftly, uninvited visions to me of sweet Audrey dressed in pink for her dance with death. Abruptly, Edmund's words wrenched me from my trance.

"I would like to ask for your daughter's hand in marriage, *Monsieur* McCord. But because of the trouble I caused in the past, I will ask that you allow me to court her proper first. With your blessing, I will stay and find work here in the city and only visit with a chaperone."

Edmund paused, hoping for more of a reaction than he'd received so far. He squirmed in his chair at the continued silence, looked at his hands to avoid the stares.

"I promise that I will be honorable in my conduct. I have great respect for you, sir," he continued.

Finally, it was Ma who mustered the courage to speak.

"Edmund, you will not get the answer here that you hope for. The news I am about to share is not good. We lost Audrey last summer, to the fever. John and Jeremy survived the illness, and then we lost baby Maureen in the winter."

Grandma looked at the table, not wanting to meet Edmund's eyes, but a dampness in Grandpa's eyes reflected the agony he saw in young Edmund's face. Grandpa could be firm, sometimes unbending and resolved once a decision was made, but there were soft spots in my grandpa that always surprised me.

"*Ce n'est pas vrai! Non.*" Tears welled in Edmund's eyes. "It cannot be. She was young . . . so filled with life." His hands covered his face. "*Non.*"

"I am sorry, son. Though I was none too happy with you last year, I can see that you loved my daughter," said Grandpa.

"She was everything, *ici*. Here." He put his hand to his chest, over his heart. "I wanted her as my wife. I saw her as the sweet mother of my children. With all my heart." Tears cut short his words, slipping down his cheeks.

In an attempt to conceal his emotions, he rose and walked outside, leaving his things behind. Through the window, we could see him wandering about the trees, at times putting his hands to his head. A couple of times, I saw his foot stomp the dirt. In anger, it seemed. My thoughts, of course, went straight to that day I could not forget, the day we buried my aunt. I am certain he was having the same thoughts I'd had last summer. If only.

"Okay, this man has traveled all this way for our Audrey. The least we can do is take him to her grave," said Grandpa. "He can sleep in the barn tonight. I guess I should ask John, but don't think he'd take well to it. Damn, I'll take him. Fidelia, you can come with us. I know you were fond of him and his Injun. Mariah, go out and tell John. Calm him down, if need be, before we all break bread this evening."

Grandpa stood and walked to his bedroom, but the rest of us sat quietly at the table. No one knew what to say, and then Ma rose and walked outside to Edmund. I am sure she told him of Grandpa's plan, invited him to supper, and sent him back inside to get his things. I followed him with Ma to the barn, where she showed him the workshop, an unused pallet sitting in the corner, covered with a small tarp to keep out the sawdust. Ma threw off the tarp, moved a small table near the bed, and laid the folded tarp on the end of Jeremy's workbench.

"Fidelia, go get some clean linens for the bedding," said Ma. She turned back to Edmund. "Fidelia will bring you a washbasin before our supper meal," she said, before walking away toward the field to find Pa.

Supper was a quiet affair. Pa had nothing to say, and Edmund, still distraught, shared a few war stories with Uncle Jeremy, stories without his customary fervor. Nevertheless, my uncle listened in wonder.

"I shoulda enlisted, right, Father?" said Uncle Jeremy.

"We lost too many, Jeremy. You were better off staying here with your family," said Edmund.

"Edmund, what made you leave your trapping and join the army?" asked Grandpa. Edmund looked down at the table, then shook his head with a slowness that went on too long. We all watched him, and I began to worry until he finally spoke.

"It was hope, sir. Hope. That I would see Audrey again. That I would survive the war to court her right. With your permission. And to defend Texas against those who *double-croix* my country, in Mexico. I fought in La Paz and then with General Lane against the guerilla fighters before the truce. I wanted to be a man worthy of your daughter."

CHAPTER 16

In the morning, after breakfast, I left with Grandpa and Edmund in our small wagon, heading east toward the morning sun, toward the cemetery near Brushy Town. When we arrived, I found there was now a proper stone, a tall McCord marker, where Grandpa had paid someone to carve the names of my aunt and my sister. A chill ran through me as I saw that there was room for more names.

Earlier that morning, after I'd milked the cow, I had gone out to the field and cut a bouquet of blue wildflowers to lay at the grave. At the cemetery, I pulled a few flowers from the bouquet and laid them at the McCord stones, then I handed the bouquet, held with a black ribbon, to Edmund and nodded. Grandpa and I walked away toward a cow pasture, allowing Edmund some time alone. I saw Edmund lay the flowers on Audrey's grave and then cross himself. I had never before thought of his faith but now believed him to be Catholic.

"As much as I disliked Edmund last year after Audrey disappeared, I must say he's a good man with bad luck," whispered Grandpa as he tamped some tobacco into his pipe and lit it with his flint.

"Now he's but a sad man," I said. I looked back at the graveyard and saw Edmund sitting there, cross-legged like his Indian friend, speaking either in prayer or to his Audrey.

"Grandpa?"

He looked down at me.

"I think we should have let her go."

I looked up at him. He looked puzzled for a moment, then his expression altered with understanding.

"Oh, Fidelia. I do think that you are a wise girl. I will tell you that such thoughts weighed heavily on me when we laid Audrey to rest. She was my daughter, only one. How were we to know God's plan for her? But you may be right."

We said no more as we stood watching the cows in the pasture, Grandpa puffing on his pipe. Finally, after some time, Edmund joined us.

"I thank you, both of you, for your kindness. *Merci*. I will be on my way this day. Back to Kansas City." He placed his hand on the top of my head, a heartfelt gesture, but the joy I'd seen yesterday upon his arrival had vanished, and I was never to see it again.

"Edmund, I wish you all the good that might come to you, in spite of all that's happened," Grandpa said. "You are certainly welcome to spend another night and leave in the morning,"

"Thank you, Monsieur McCord. You are a generous man, but I will head north toward my home. Your family has been more than kind to me."

As we traveled back on the trail, Grandpa and Edmund quietly talked about the war, and I heard stories of fierce battles and near death. It came clear to me that Edmund had truly risked his own life to see my aunt again, to earn our regard. I sat between the two men, now as awestruck by Edmund as I had been by Gray Feather.

When we reached home, Grandma packed some dried

turkey and cornbread for Edmund's journey, refilled his canteen with fresh water from the well, and, with his horse refreshed and packed, he left us.

Jeremy's and Pa's labor and Grandpa's persistence, having been met with a wet spring and a bit of summer rain, made 1848 a good year. In the morning, through the summer and into fall, Ma and I helped the men in the fields. I carried small bales of cotton and baskets of potatoes and onions to the barn in spite of summer's heat, and there ended up being enough profit to purchase some horses. Emily and I made friends at the church, and my new friend, Rosa Brandt, lived nearby and had visited my home once.

When my chores and lessons were done, I would run over to the Brandt farm, where lines and lines of cotton plants stood in formation like brigades of soldiers. Rosa told me that the farmhands out in the fields were slaves.

"Really, only two of them," she said. "The others are temporary field hands my Papa hires to help. My ma wants our slaves freed, but my papa has not yet done so. That lady, over there in the old bentwood chair, is the grandmother of Abe out there in the field. She is ninety-seven years old, and Ma no longer allows her to work."

I looked across the grass, past the trees, at the old woman in the chair. Her hair was white and pulled into a frayed bun. Her dark, golden-brown skin set off her eyes as she stared back at me, then slowly nodded her head at us. Intrigue filled me.

"Fidelia, come meet my parents," said Rosa, and she dragged me toward her house, a large, white stone home with a long porch she called a veranda. Rosa's mother was in the kitchen, standing at the basin, and a large man whom I'd seen at church, her pa, sat at the table. Rosa's mother set a plate of beans in front of the man, but he said nothing to us, and only smiled at Rosa's ma.

"Mama, this is my friend Fidelia. Remember, from the church? She lives on that farm near ours."

Rosa's mother smiled at me, revealing a sparkle in her eyes. Her skin was sun-kissed, and her hair, as dark as coal, hung straight down her back. She greeted me with a strong accent, and I wondered if she was an Indian like my friend Gray Feather. Rosa's father barely raised his head when I was introduced, and he greeted me with only a grunt. I was not sure if I liked him. Brightly painted crucifixes, like the ones on my ma's rosary beads, dressed the wall behind Mr. Brandt.

"Can we play, Mama? Out by the barn?" asked Rosa.

"Not now, *mi corazón*. You have your chores." Missus Brandt smiled at me and looked at Rosa. I was pondering what name she had called my friend.

"I'll walk home. Maybe I can come back tomorrow," I said, then hugged Rosa and left.

I walked toward home, toward the old lady in the chair.

"G'day, sweet girl," she said.

I smiled and stopped in my tracks, for I had been eager to visit with her.

"My friend Rosa told me you are ninety-seven years old. That means you were born in the 1700s," I said, pausing to do the math in my head. "In 1751."

"I think so, girl. So long ago, I don't remember."

"I'm Fidelia. My granny calls me Delia."

I gathered the fullness of my skirt and sat in the grass

near the old woman.

"Good ta meet you, Fidelia. 'Tis a pretty name. You can call me Granny. 'Tis what everyone calls me now."

"My granny lives with us. She came to Texas with us from Indiana. Why is your Abe, your grandson, a slave?" I said, nodding out toward the workers in the fields.

"Mercy, little girl, you do go right to the meddling, don't ya?"

I stared at her, still awaiting an answer.

"Girl. My chil'ren were born that way. Born slaves. Just like me. Some days I think they no different than the ones, Jim and Saul, out there in the field gettin' paid."

"Why?"

"You nosy, like a cat." She paused, looking out over the fields. "My Abe still gets his meals, a roof 'bove his head. The missus is good to us. The master is at times gruff, like his pa, who bought me off a selling platform in Galveston. But Master Brandt, like his pa, never raised a hand to us, like I seen 'fore coming here."

"I don't understand why a being can own another being. I think God would not like that," I said to the old woman, who, to me at that moment, seemed wiser than anyone I knew, except maybe Gray Feather.

"Well, girl, you a lot like our missus. She think just like you."

I stood. "You know, maybe the new president will end this slavery. I heard my grandpa talking about it, so the government must wanna fix it."

"Honey, that ain't gonna happen in my lifetime."

I paused and looked at the old woman, pondering her words. "I better get on home. Before dinner."

"Well, Delia, girl, you can come back and visit me

anytime. I think I like you . . . you is like a sweet pepper. An' Rosa . . . Rosa can always use a friend 'cause her brother is grown an' gone."

I smiled and waved at the old lady as I walked away. I did not even know her name but knew she had lived lots of life and likely had seen much hardship having been confined to a realm of obligation and toil. I had already decided that I would visit her again.

CHAPTER 17

It was that summer in 1848 when Grandpa hired a vagrant to help harvest the cotton and vegetables. Seth was a young man, near Uncle Jeremy's age, and he lived by drifting through the wilderness, rootless, catching odd jobs for a bit of money and food. To me, it seemed a life akin to that of the fur traders, except Seth worked as he chose. Though he'd looked ragged when he showed up, he turned out to be a hard worker, and it wasn't long before Grandma's cooking and Ma's stitching had Seth looking like a gentleman fit to court one's daughter. As it turned out, it was a good thing that we had no such marriageable daughters.

Seth had a deck of cards, and on some evenings after supper, he taught Emily and me how to play a game he called Twenty-One. Said he'd learned it on a ship. Jeremy joined us once or twice in the game and told us it was a gambling game. That would explain why Grandma frowned when she saw us playing cards, or maybe it was more about us playing cards with Seth. She'd often call us into the house before our game was finished, saying she needed some help in the kitchen.

All the men worked long hours into fall, yet Grandpa would still sneak off to the river to fish and Pa still held tight to his anger. One morning, near the end of October, Uncle Jeremy was missing at the breakfast table, and no one knew where he was. By evening, Grandpa was pacing the floor.

"Something's happened. Seth wasn't here today. Doesn't look like he slept in the barn last night. What are the two of 'em up to?" said Grandpa, more to himself than to anyone in the room.

"Jeremy won't do nothing stupid," said Grandma. "Don't know about Seth, but Jeremy wouldn't just leave, saying nothing, not come home."

It was two more days before my uncle and Seth came dragging down the path, heads bent and looking no one in the eye. Seth had a shiner, and Jeremy was limping. Both had scrapes on their faces starting to scab over, and I could tell they'd been fighting.

"Where have you boys been?" asked Grandpa as he walked out of the barn, his usual calm absent from his voice.

"In jail, Father. Got in a fight," said Jeremy.

"I can see that. What was the fight about?"

"We drank too much, sir," said Seth. "Got in a brawl with some fella from San Antonio, then his friends joined in. Didn't end till the sheriff showed up."

"Where were you both? You still haven't told me what you were fighting about. And, Seth, you no longer work here. The harvesting's near done. Get your stuff and move on."

Seth huffed toward the barn, leaving his horse behind, and Grandpa turned to look at me.

"Fidelia, go tell your Grandma that Jeremy is home," he said.

As I walked toward the house, I saw Grandpa and Jeremy leading the horses into the barn, and I could see

Grandpa shaking his head as Jeremy talked. It's not likely I'll ever know what started that fight, even if he did tell Grandpa.

Early the next morning, Jeremy walked into the barn as I sat on the old stool, milking the cow. He looked startled to see me, which was odd given I sat just like this on the stool each morning, watching the warm milk spurt from the cow's swollen udder.

"Delia," he said, as if I'd surprised him, as if I didn't know who I was.

"Jeremy, what were ya thinking?" I said. "Going off like that with Seth? I bet Grandpa's still mad at ya for scaring us."

"I'm tired of being nobody around here. It's like John says. We're just indentured workers, but at least Father lets John be. He treats me like I'm a young'un."

I pulled the full bucket out from under the cow and just stared at Jeremy. My mind wandered to yesterday, and the question about the fight was on the tip of my tongue when Jeremy spoke again.

"I can never measure up. In Father's eyes, it's always Levi and John he counts on. Levi's the best farmer he's ever seen. John solves every problem he's sent to fix. Never me. No one respects me," whined Jeremy as he kicked at the wall and then pulled a bale of hay out for the horses.

I didn't know what to say to my uncle because I believed he might be right. He was the family's errand boy, like one of us, the grandchildren.

"I count on you, Uncle Jeremy," I said, not believing my words would carry enough weight to make a difference. But as he lifted the hay bale, my uncle looked at me with a loving compassion that revealed my words had mattered, and before I carried the milk to the kitchen, I walked over and tried to hug my uncle with that bulky bale of hay between us, and then we both broke into laughter. I had succeeded in lifting his mood, if nothing else beyond.

On most Sundays, Emily and I went to church services with Ma and Grandma. Grandpa and Uncle Jeremy would come with us when their field work allowed. If I couldn't grab the seat next to Grandpa, I would sit next to Uncle Jeremy, nudging him to sing along with us from the hymnal. He'd playfully nudge me back but still remain silent or merely mouth the song's words. I never knew if my uncle could sing or not.

On Sunday afternoons I would sometimes go to the Brandt farm to spend time with my friend Rosa, even though I usually saw her at church. Ma expected me to play with my sister, so I visited Rosa when I could get away alone for a bit. Once Emily went with me, and we all played hide and seek in the barn until we almost lost Emily out in the cotton fields. She came home with scratches all over her ankles, and after that day she was no longer eager to follow me across the fields to visit my friend.

I still went with Grandma, one or two days each week, to the market, and with the money from those sales added to the profits from our crops, we had replaced all of our lost horses. Grandpa bought a few more chickens and even had enough money to make some improvements to the house. He said that with one more good year, he would purchase a handsome plow for the farm and perhaps offer to buy the farm itself. The crop fields were near cleared and readied for next year, but most of the talk was about the election of 1848.

"That damn Whig party has spun on its heel with that Mexican War officer, Taylor, running for office. After all their talk of Polk's warmongering, they're sputtering fools," said Pa at the dinner table.

"I think I'm going to vote with the Green Soils, for Van Buren," said Jeremy, his voice filled with a rare confidence.

"Why is that, son?" asked Grandpa.

"Because Van Buren's opposing the system . . . and he's against Cass," said Jeremy.

"Is Buren the one that's gonna make the slaves free?" I asked.

Everyone looked at me, and the room grew quiet as a church meeting when the preacher spoke of tithes.

"If that's so, I've decided that's who I'm voting for. Buren," I said.

"For the good of God, girl. You can't vote. Only men can vote. Grown men," said Pa, sticking a fork into his last piece of ham. I pulled a face and threw my thoughts to the food on my own plate.

"Fidelia, you are right," said Grandpa. "Van Buren, an old Democrat barnburner, is against swelling the slavery in our new land. They, the Green Soil party, are the only ones speaking out against it. But, sadly, he will not win the election . . . he'll just throw the votes to the Whigs. Though I do believe General Taylor will be a good leader for our country at this time."

Grandma smiled at Grandpa, suggesting her agreement.

"This Van Buren man . . . he burns barns?" I asked. It seemed an odd thing for a man wanting to be president to do.

Pa threw me an exasperated look, Jeremy chuckled, and

Emily's eyes grew wide at hearing my question.

"No, dear. That is a name the people call the Democrats who are rebellious about their party tolerating slavery. They are the ones who are now backing Van Buren," said Grandma. "It's like a nickname."

My thoughts wandered away from the conversation at the table because all the words and contradictions dismissed my interest in politics. All I could think of was how much I hated that I would have to tell the old Negro woman at Rosa's that she was probably right. She would not be free in her lifetime.

The first Tuesday in November turned out to be a gray and chilly day, but Grandpa put on his Sunday suit, the one he wore to funerals and sometimes to church, and he called for Jeremy and Pa to get ready to go vote in Austin.

"I ain't votin'. No use in it," said Pa. "There's work to do around here . . . need to turn the harvested fields."

"Son, that can wait. However, it is your choice not to go . . . Just don't complain about who wins or loses."

I was fairly certain that Grandpa's warning would not stop the complaining from my pa. Uncle Jeremy walked into the kitchen dressed in a clean shirt and he grabbed his jacket from the hook. Now twenty, he was a handsome young man dressed up and shaven. I watched Grandma pull a scarf around her son's neck and knot it tight.

"For the chill, son," said Grandma.

The two men left on their horses, riding away on a glum day toward the trail to Austin, where I was certain they would likely cancel out each other's vote. The skies were beginning to darken when they returned, and Grandpa, without a word to anyone, walked to the barn with his horse and came out with his fishing pole and bait basket. He walked away in the direction of the pond. I knew it wasn't a good time for fishing, so, clearly, he had a wont for some quiet time. I wondered what had happened in Austin City.

The unmasking to my wonder came at supper, when I heard Jeremy, in a muted voice, tell Pa that he'd gotten into a fight at the voting place.

"Two cotton farmers from out in the country challenged me when they heard me talking to Pa about my vote. Said no Negro lovers are welcome in their state, and they started pushing me around, so I slugged the big one. Next thing I knew, they had me on the ground, pounding me. I fought back, kicking and biting, which only made them punch me harder, till Pa pulled the two of them off me."

"Who looked worse? You?" said Pa.

"Yeah, me. Though I bloodied the nose on one of 'em."

"A circus," said Pa. "Knew I shouldn't go. These elections are nothing but a damned carnival."

I looked closer and could see why Jeremy still had on his hat, his brim pulled down low. My uncle's left eye was swelled like a week-old plum, and I could see blood by his eyebrow. It was clear he had whispered his tale so that Grandma wouldn't hear about it, but I knew he wouldn't be able to hide that puffy shiner for long. It was at that moment, when Grandma sat down to eat with us, that Grandpa walked in.

"Evening," said Grandpa.

It was dark outside, and he arrived empty-handed, but

that was no surprise to me.

"No fish biting at the pond. What's for supper?" he asked as he sat at the table.

"Chicken and dumplings, and some succotash and corn pones," answered Grandma. Grandpa looked over at Jeremy.

"Son, take off that hat. You're at the supper table," said Grandpa as Grandma scooped some chicken and dumplings onto his plate.

Jeremy scowled and looked down as he removed his hat, balancing it on the back corner of his chair. It wasn't long before Grandma and Ma noticed his face.

"What happened to you?" asked Grandma, looking back and forth between her youngest son and Grandpa. "You need to wash that, put some iodine on it."

"Well, son, I'll let you explain that to your mother," said Grandpa, turning his attention to the meal set before him.

I could tell Jeremy soft-soaped the story, telling Grandma it was nothing. Grandpa's raised eyebrows and the squint of his eyes when he looked over at Jeremy verified my suspicion. Soon enough, Grandma was gathering a washbowl and a rag and dragging her youngest son off to a stool near the hearth.

It came clear to me that evening that politics was a place for discretion, and it was no small matter in the course of events and in the bonds of family.

Chapter 18

Just before the Christmas season, cold winds and freezing temperatures blew through the farm, but when a warm day came, I walked slowly, step by step, over to Rosa's house. Our school lessons in the morning had been short because of the holiday, and I carried a gift Ma was sending with me, a pecan and spice cake she had baked for the Brandts, so I stepped cautiously, weaving around the shrubs and cottonwoods to the meadow now withered by winter at the edge of the Brandt farm.

"Rosa," I called out as I knocked at the neighbor's front door. "Missus Brandt?"

It was Rosa who opened the door, and I handed the cake to her mother, who stood behind her.

"Thank you. *Gracias, gracias*, Fidelia," said Missus Brandt, and she turned to set the cake on the grand oak table embellished with intricate carvings along the edges. "Did you bake this?"

"No," I said, then giggled. I had not yet learned to bake cakes or pies. "Ma made the cake. For you."

"You tell your mother that I send my blessings and gratitude for the cake. It smells so good. You will tell her, and not forget?" she asked.

I nodded. "Can Rosa play outside with me, Missus Brandt?"

"Yes, dear. But first, let me feed you girls. Some soup.

Are you hungry?" she said, looking at me.

"Yes, ma'am."

"I made a big pot of pea soup, and I'll bring some bread. And it is almost Christmas, so some *champurrado. Si*?"

I did not always understand Missus Brandt's words, but I smiled and sat with Rosa at the big table. A large bowl of green soup was delivered to each of us with a basket of biscuits, still warm. The soup was delicious and laced with a bit more spice than the pea soup Ma made for us at home. When we had almost finished, Rosa's ma set two small, red clay bowls before us filled with a warm dark liquid unlike any I'd seen before. I watched as Rosa raised the bowl to her lips and I followed her example. My first sip filled my mouth with the taste of chocolate, a hot chocolate that coated my tongue and eased its way down my throat, leaving behind only a sweet warmth that made me want more.

"This is so good," I said, taking the cotton napkin and wiping my mouth.

"Mama's family is from Mexico," Rosa said. "They have a large ranch near the Rio Grande, a majestic place that was built by my grandfather's parents before him. It is where my papa met Mama during the revolution. My grandparents, whom I have not seen since I was around four or five years old, were not at all happy when Mama fell in love with my pa, with a warrior from the north country, come to take Mexican lands. Mama tells the story all the time of their secret love and how they met each other when she was riding her horse along the river, where Pa saw her. My pa told me she was a beautiful *señorita*, with her black hair tied at the nape of her neck and a smile that almost made him fall off his horse as he turned to watch her. Then he stopped and watched her, gazing like a lovelorn fool . . . those were my pa's words. After that, they would meet by the river and talk as they rode along the water. After the war was done, he properly courted Ma and then they wed. Now, my grandparents love Pa." Rosa took another sip of her *champurrado*.

"She is very beautiful, your mama. Why does she call you Cora and not Rosa?"

"Oh. Not Cora. It's *corazón. Mi corazón* in Spanish means 'my dear heart.' It is a phrase of affection that she uses," said Rosa.

"Oh," I said. I finished my chocolate drink and, following Rosa, carried the bowl to Missus Brandt in the kitchen. "Thank you, Missus Brandt. This is the sweetest drink I've ever had. Maybe, one day, you can teach my ma to make it."

"Oh, *mi corazón,* yes, I can," she said.

I smiled at her as I handed her my bowl, feeling as if I were family.

"What is the old Negro woman's name, the one who sits under the tree?" I asked Rosa as we walked toward their barns.

"Oh, that's Abby. She used to help my ma in the kitchen when I was a little girl; now she just sits by the field and watches her grandson work during the planting season, watches the crops grow or the work get done."

Rosa pointed to small buildings beyond the barn.

"The slaves live over there in those two cottages, and sometimes Mama will send food out to them. But they do have an old kitchen in that cabin there," Rosa said, pointing to the one nearest the barn. "On cold and rainy days, Abby stays in their kitchen. My mama cannot read much English, but my older brother used to sit and read the news to Abby and her grandson Abe, or so Abe once told me."

"Maybe I could read to her from my school reader," I said.

"Why would you do that?" asked Rosa.

"Because she might like that. And someday, when I'm a better reader, I could read to her from the Bible."

"Don't be silly. When would we play? Let's go find the goats in the little barn, or maybe they're out in the field," said Rosa.

We found the goats in the cleared field and sat amongst them as the animals ate crop remnants and weeds. The young ones would walk over to us, press our shoulders, and run around before returning to their meals.

"So, is your mama a Catholic, like my ma was as a girl?" I asked.

"Yes, she is, but we go to our church 'cause Papa is Lutheran, like his parents who came to this country from Germany. Mama now is a Lutheran too, though I sometimes see her with her rosary, and she crosses herself with her hand, like the shape of a cross."

"My ma too," I said.

My heart warmed at being blessed to have a friend like Rosa who understood me, who was, in some ways, like me. I could talk to her about how my pa had changed and was often angry, and Rosa told me how her pa said little to her. She said it was his German ways, and then she shared how he doted on her mama. How sometimes she would see them dancing in the late evening candlelight, swaying around the big dining table; and, as I listened to her stories, a regret settled in my chest that my own parents were now so lost. It made me sad that, each day, my ma withdrew into a new loneliness, even in the midst of family.

When Missus Brandt called from the porch for Rosa to come home, I said my goodbyes and walked towards old Abby, who sat in her chair by the trees.

"Good day, Miss Abby," I said.

"Well, well, girl. I see ya learned my name. Miss Delia, isn't it?"

"Yes, it is. A nice sunny day for winter, ain't it? Is that why you're sitting out here?"

"Yes ma'am," she said. I was surprised she called me ma'am.

"Guess that's what brought you out. The sun? Will you be helpin' your mama fixin' the Christmas supper? Comin' soon," asked Abby.

"I suppose I will be helping a little. Sometimes Em and I just have to stay out of the way."

"You have a li'l sister?" asked Abby.

"Yes. Her name is Emily, but I call her Em. She's six years old, so Mama has started schooling her."

"You is a lucky girl, Delia, to have a sister. Little Rosa don't but is lucky havin' a friend. You."

I looked at her in silence. Little did she know that I'd had two more sisters, now resting in graves, but I chose not to share the sorrows. I had no doubts that this lady had seen a lifetime of her own sadness.

"Yes, Miss Abby, you are right about friends and sisters. I love my time with Rosa. You know, my grandpa and uncle voted in the election, and there was a man Grandpa said was against the slavery. A Mister Buren, I think, but he didn't win the election. I would've voted for him if I could've, but I'm a girl. I was sad for you when Grandpa told me Mister Buren lost that election, Miss Abby."

"Oh, dear sweet girl, no need to be. This is the life I got. Soon 'nuf I'll join my own daughter in the heaven. No need to feel bad for me."

"But I want your grandson to be a free man. I will pray every day that will happen for him. And I wish I could come read the Bible to you. Maybe I will," I said.

"I remember when Hans, Rosa's brother, used to read to me all the time. Hans was born when Master Brandt was married to his first wife. The first missus was a frail lady, always sickly, and died when Hans was but three. Hans would read news when I worked in the kitchen, and sometimes he'd read me a rhyme. Sweet boy. But willful. S'pose that's why he has such a big plantation now, over to the east. Abe's gone to work for him a time or two."

"Rosa told me he used to read to you, but I have never met her brother." I sprung up from the ground, brushed the dry grass from my skirt, and stood next to Abby. "But I will read to you. The next time I come here. I must go home for the supper meal, but I'll visit you on the next warm day, when I can come over."

"God willin', girl. Bless you for visitin' with me," said Abby as her frail hand ran down my sleeve in a gentle gesture. I bent over and hugged her, softly, for I feared she might break, and I walked away toward home.

I walked slowly, my thoughts swirling in my head like flocks of starlings that swarmed into clouds made of birds. My heart embraced my new friends, Rosa and Abby. I wondered what had happened to Miss Abby's daughter. I was filled with a joy of being welcomed into Rosa's family as I ambled around the cedar shrubs between our farms, hearing only the crackle of my steps on the dry, brown sward of winter.

I learned later that the sweet boy Abby spoke of, Hans, had turned hard when he grew older and fought in the Mexican War, the very war my friend Edmund had returned from.

At supper that evening, I was thinking of my visit with Abby when Grandpa started with one of his stories, a story that leapt right out of my own day across the meadow at the Brandt farm.

"When I was just a boy," said Grandpa, "near the fort, I'd sometimes sit and talk with an old Indian woman, a Miami, I believe she was, the mother or grandmother of one of the fort's Indian translators who'd come in with some fur traders one day and never left. This old woman was sad that she was no longer with her tribe, but she always reminded me to thank my god for every sunrise. She had come from a place called Kekionga near the St. Joseph River, and I'll never forget the food she cooked and sometimes shared with me at the fort. She could take a squirrel and cook it tender with the tastiest squash she grew in her own garden and the flavors would echo on your tongue like a tune. Linger for a time. Who knew squirrels could be so delicious, but later I came to know it was how she spiced the squash and cooked it all together. I remember once asking my ma to make such a meal, and she looked at me in horror. But I will, with certainty, never forget old Running Bird."

"Her name was Running Bird?" asked Emily.

"She told me that the tribe named her Running Bird when she was young, tiny, and began walking, fast as one of them roadrunners we see here in Texas. She was walking while other babes were yet on their knees."

My thoughts went to how much like my grandpa I was. We both had befriended Indians, drawn to them with an awe of their ways. I prayed that night that I would always have a big heart like my Grandpa.

CHAPTER 19

In January I turned nine, and with that, Pa decided it was time for me to take on more chores.

"You're old enough now, Fidelia, to start helping with the garden and clean the outhouse," he said. "Along with milking the cow in the morning and churning the butter, you can help your ma weed and plant the vegetable garden. Next year you can start helping with the crop harvest."

"Yes, sir," I said.

"You'll not have the girls cleaning that outhouse, John. Not when there are able-bodied men around here to do that chore. You and Jeremy can trade off on it. What you've given her to do is enough without that," said Grandma in her firm, I-mean-it voice. I gave a large sigh of relief on the inside, so no one could see or hear it. It was terrifying enough to use the outhouse in the dark night, let alone scrub it down.

"Pa, I can keep the bin filled. With the lime," I said, hoping that would appease him.

"Good enough," he said, looking over at Grandma. She said nothing, so it was decided.

After Pa left the house, Grandma told me to always tie a bandana around my nose and mouth when shoveling the lime.

"No good breathing in that stuff, Delia," she said.

From then on, once a week, I shoveled lime into the

wheelbarrow and pushed it to the outhouse, then scooped it into the bin next to the stack of old corncobs. Once I'd forgotten to tie a rag about my face, but I never made that mistake again, for I coughed mightily into the night.

I knew education was important to Ma, but there were no teachers near our farm, so Ma decided she would continue mathematics and reading studies for Emily and me at home. Ma and Pa would have to work that out on their own, for Pa saw little use in educating girls. The spring garden wouldn't start until the end of February or in March, so there was still time to visit with Rosa and old Abby over at the Brandt farm.

The summer crops grew well, and as summer ended, Grandpa had bartered for three pigs, one for eatin' and two for making more pigs. Now that the swine were healthy, happy, and fattened up, Pa and Grandpa decided it was time for some sausage and pork ribs. Emily ran when she heard the squealing coming from behind the barn, squeals that pierced the air around me with such vibrations that even the trees likely shook. I stood watching Emily vanish into the house and was torn between my own fear and curiosity. As I rounded the barn, I saw the pig hanging lifeless, blood running into a pot. The blood gushed from where they'd sliced his neck, and as I stood slack-jawed, it dwindled to a trickle. Through the day, I saw Grandma running to the barn with pots, and there were pork ribs for supper that evening.

I must say, I was sickened, almost to the verge of retching, when I walked into the barn the next morning to milk the cow, only to find pig intestines strung from the low rafters and a large barrel of salt with bits of pig guts lying within. But with all the drama of the day before, the savory fragrance of bacon in Grandma's kitchen lured me to the table.

Ma decided in October that it was a good time for me to learn how to use the spinning wheel. I discovered it was not an easy task to learn, but if I mastered spinning the yarn from wool and some cotton, my ma and grandma would have more yarn to weave and knit into gloves and scarves. Ma was patient with me as I practiced spinning the wheel in the correct direction and pulling taut the yarn from the bobbin. Emily watched, often in robust laughter, as I struggled to grow my skill. I was awkward, dropping the spindle, tangling the threads in the bobbin, and clumsy at throwing the wheel. In the end, I was not fond of the art of spinning wool or cotton. I did, however, continue working on my stitching talents and eventually I mastered tatting under my mother's guidance.

Tatting, like fishing, was a meditation, and I found its repetitiveness to be calming. Once I finished a piece, I would work the cotton lace onto collars of dresses Ma had sewn, or on sleeves and on embroidered hankies. I embellished new muslin chemises for Grandma, Ma, Emily, and myself.

With the soft sunlight of late autumn evenings, I'd often take the dark pillow Ma had made for me, along with sturdy threads, netting needles, and bobbins, and sit outside, leaving Ma indoors with her spinning wheel or other chores. I could sit under the tree until the sky began to dim, with Bear snuggled at my feet, making fine lace for Ma to use. It was like Grandpa and his fishing pole, like absorbing our own selves into a trance. My friend Rosa would sit in awe of my skill, and her mother asked me if I would make her some lace for her to stitch on a new shawl, which I promptly did.

One day Ma had some extra fabric she said I could have, a bit of green wool that was long enough for me to finish hems for a warm wrap and edge with my fine lace. I made this shawl for Abby, and I could not wait to give it to her.

Winter came upon us in December, with its slower pace and barren fields, waiting for the next spring. My morning chores were done late one morning, and I decided to carry my gift over to Abby. She was not sitting aside the fields, as it was still winter and the fields were empty. I walked up to Rosa's house and knocked. Missus Brandt answered the door and invited me in.

"My, my, girl, it is cold outside. Rosa is in the kitchen. Come in. Come sit down at the table, and I'll bring you a coffee. Take your cloak off."

"I am not permitted to drink coffee, Missus Brandt," I said.

"Then I will bring you some apple cider. Let me heat it up, and Rosa will join you when she has put the dishes away."

As I sat down at the table, I draped my cloak on the back of the chair and laid my folded gift and my book on the chair beside me. The house was joyfully quiet, with occasional sounds of faint clinking coming from the kitchen. I sat quiet, enjoying the repose around me.

After a time, Missus Brandt walked in with a tray and her daughter behind her.

"Here you go, girls," she said.

There was a bowl of cider for each of us, Rosa and me,

and Missus Brandt set a plate of pones and cookies on the table.

"Thank you, Missus Brandt," I said.

Rosa and I sat, drinking and eating and giggling, for quite some time. I loved being at my friend's home, where I found warmth and peacefulness that seemed absent at my own home, where gloom and conflict lodged.

"Mama is getting kitchen help again. Abe has taken a wife, a negotiated trade from my brother's farm, where Abe met her, and she will help Mama in the kitchen. She is quite sweet. Reka. That's her name."

"So, is she a slave, now that she is married to Abe?" I asked.

"Yes, silly. She gets on well with Mama and wants to learn Ma's recipes from Mexico."

"Is Abby at their cabin? I brought a gift for her," I said.

"What did you bring her?"

"I made her a shawl, though winters here are so short. She can use it when she needs some warmth." I lifted it from the chair to show her the color.

"I suppose she is at the cabin, probably cooking for the men. But she naps quite often. We'll walk over there," said Rosa.

We put our dishes on the tray and walked into the kitchen.

"Mama, Fidelia has a gift for Abby. I'll go out to the cabins with her so she can share her gift."

"How generous of you, Fidelia. That is fine, Rosa. Your Papa will be home soon, so you can come back later and help in the kitchen."

The cabin near the barn was dark. A young Negro woman was cooking in the kitchen. The men were not there but working in the barn, likely feeding the animals and raking the stalls.

"Fidelia, this is Reka, Abe's new wife," said Rosa by way of introduction. Reka was not tall, but slender, her hair tied in a faded yellow scarf, and she had the most striking eyes and a warm smile.

"It is good to meet you, Fidelia. I know Rosa is happy to have a friend. I just finished making a ham and pea soup. Would you girls like some?"

"Thank you, but no. We just ate in Missus Brandt's kitchen. Is Abby here?" I asked.

"She is lying down. Let me go get her."

"Oh, no, don't wake her," I said.

"I don't believe she is sleeping. I'll get her," said Reka, and she was gone in a flash.

I looked around at their meager space. This cabin was for Abe and his wife and his grandmother, but it had a kitchen. The other help stayed in the second cabin. Reka had returned to the stove, and I heard the tap-tap of Abby's cane as she entered the room.

"Oh, girls, I don't much have visitors. So, who are you?" she said to me as she walked toward us.

"I am Fidelia," I replied, confused that she did not know me. But when she got near, her eyes lit with recognition.

"Oh, dear child. Yes, Delia. How sweet of you and Rosa to come visit."

I helped Abby into one of the chairs by the small dining table and handed her the shawl I'd made. "This is a gift for you. I made it to keep you warm," I said.

Abby slowly unfolded the green shawl, and I saw her hands tremble.

"Oh, my. My! You made this, Delia? So pretty. Did ya make the lace, girl?" asked Abby.

"Yes, ma'am," I said. "But my ma helped me color it." We had used winter greens from the garden to color the cotton threads.

"You is smart. And look at this! You sewed a bird, a sweet bluebird here in the corner. Your 'broider is so pretty, Delia."

The old woman lifted the fabric to her cheek, savoring its snug softness as she held it there and closed her eyes.

"It is 'most too pretty to wear," said Abby.

"No, ma'am. You must wear it every day, when you are chilled. It is for every day. For now."

Abby looked into my eyes, held them in silence until it seemed nearly awkward.

"I told you. You is wise. I know well I may not be here next year, or next week, so I best wear it now," she said.

I help place the shawl over Abby's shoulders, and she looked toward Rosa.

"Dear girl, you have a sweet friend here. You are both blessed girls. As am I, knowin' ya."

She reached her arms to hug Rosa and then me, and in spite of her frailty, I found her hugs to be warm and deep.

"Abby, I also brought my reader so that I can read you some of my lessons. Next week I'll bring my Bible 'cause those are the only two books I have," I said.

"Goodness, girl. Let me hear ya read."

I sat reading to Abby while Rosa ate muffins and drank coffee in the kitchen with Reka. It wasn't long before Abby fell asleep in her chair, and Reka helped her back to bed. I grabbed a muffin as Rosa and I left.

The sun was lowering in the west when we ran back

into Rosa's house, and I heard singing in the kitchen. It was a woman's voice singing words I did not understand, and when we walked into the big kitchen, Rosa's mama and papa were dancing round the room. Missus Brandt's voice was soft and melodic, and her husband spun her around as she closed her eyes and sang. When I looked at Rosa, she was smiling, and when her mama opened her eyes, she winked at us as she stepped in step with her husband around the kitchen, round and round her bread table.

I must say that I was surprised to see gruff old Mister Brandt dancing, and though I did not want to leave this happy place, I needed to get home to help Grandma with supper.

CHAPTER 20

"Mama?" I said one afternoon when we were both doing some embroidery by the window. Ma was showing my sister how to make a cross-stitch.

"Yes, dear?"

"You should visit Missus Brandt one day. You know, Rosa's mother, from church. I think you would be good friends."

"Really. Why do you think that?" replied Ma.

"Well, she likes to cook and makes the sweetest chocolate drink. And she likes to dance. She is quite sweet to the slaves. They have four now, since Abe has a bride. One is too old to still work."

Ma smiled at me. "Is she the one you made the lovely shawl for? The old woman?" she asked.

"Yes. And she wears it, always, when there's a chill."

"That was kind of you, Fidelia. Isn't that right, Em?"

Emily nodded as she focused intently on her stitches.

"I do have little free time to visit, but I shall take your counsel, Fidelia. We'll take her some berries from our garden in spring, or a tart. And I must take one to Missus Brown, who has been so kind to us since we came."

Though Emily and I spent much of our days with Ma or Grandma, helping with the women's work, Pa's disappointments had carried him farther away from us. He would work during the day with Grandpa, readying the fields for planting, but sometimes he missed our family meal in the evening and came home late after everyone had gone to bed. At times I'd hear harsh words between him and Ma in the middle of the night, and Pa would not be at breakfast. There was no discretion in this house, within our paltry walls.

"Son, you must try to make a success here in our new home. You father is worried, and your family needs you, John," said Grandma one morning after everyone had left the breakfast table and I was washing dishes at the basin.

"I'll deal with it, but I don't see any success in this damned place. I don't know why we ever left our home in Indiana," said Pa.

"Because your father saw dreams in this new land, son. Prospects were fading back home. We are happy here. Why can't you be? It does take time to grow a new home. Be patient, John. And I fear your Mariah is lonely in her marriage. She needs you, John."

Pa looked none too happy with this counsel and said no more before he rose to join his father and brother in the field. I spent the rest of the morning with Ma, pulling weeds and working the soil, preparing for the coming spring. Afterwards, Ma gave us our daily instruction at the big table, my readings and essays and Emily's reading and math problems.

As the year passed, Pa was absent more and more often, and sometimes Uncle Jeremy would head to town with his older brother. The toll on Grandpa, through planting season, could be seen clear in his eyes, his sagging shoulders in the mornings, and it made me sad, but I was but a child and could not fix it. Nor did I truly understand it. It was a sultry July morning as I finished milking the cows . . . now we had two of them. I joined Grandpa and Uncle Jeremy in the workshop, where I found them sanding the slats for a small wagon they were crafting to use about the farm.

"Are you ready for a fishing trip, Fidelia? I think it's still early enough to catch something," asked Grandpa. "This chore can wait. Jeremy, I'll leave it to you."

"Yes, let's go. I'll get my pole. Wait, Grandpa, I'll go dig up some worms in the garden," I said.

As I grabbed my fishing basket, I heard Grandpa invite Jeremy to come with us. I ran to the garden with a spade and returned to the barn, having thrown at least eight fat worms into my basket. Grandpa was ready, having saddled his horse, and I handed him the bait basket before he pulled me up on the saddle behind him.

"Is Jeremy going with us?" I asked.

"Nope. Said he'd finish up the wagon while we're gone," said Grandpa. "We'll have better luck at the river," He turned the horse toward the west. "And besides, we can stay longer." Grandpa turned to smile at me.

Grandpa had a special spot at the edge of the river where he kept an old, anchored dinghy. We climbed in, and Grandpa rowed upstream toward a grove of trees that blocked the rising morning sun.

"We might find some bass hiding under the water here," he whispered.

We were quiet and waited. I was the first one to get a bite and pull in a bass, fat and shiny enough for our supper, for most all of us. Before the breezes turned hot, Grandpa and I each caught a perch. A fine meal to bring home to Grandma.

"Grandpa, I love the quiet time on the river. Don't you?"

"I sure do. Gives me time to ponder what crops to plant next," he said.

I laughed out loud, then I wondered if he truly did think about that.

"I wonder where that blue heron is going," I said, pointing at the one flying near us. "And I wonder if that skinny egret over there is getting enough to eat, and why the finches are chirping. And if there's a snake lurking in that tree."

With those last words of mine, I shuddered.

"Never had a snake drop into the boat," said Grandpa. "But I suppose there's always a first time."

Upon hearing those words, I shuddered again.

"Do you want to share these perch with that white egret over there?" asked Grandpa, trying to hold back his grin.

"No, Grandpa." We both started laughing, so loud that we surely scared away any fish swimming near us and the egret took to the sky.

We did not stay at the river as long as we would have liked, once the near-noon sun brought the heat of the day and drove us home. I returned to my school lessons, and Grandpa returned to the workshop in the barn. Pa did not come home until the following day, a Saturday.

Before I had dressed to milk the cows, I heard the yelling coming from Ma's room downstairs. I didn't hear all being said, but I could tell that Ma was mad and did not pause enough to catch her breath or allow Pa to say anything. I heard words like *carousing* and *indiscreet*, and something about leading Jeremy astray. I didn't know the meaning of all that I heard, but the fray woke everyone in the house except Emily.

By the time I walked down the stairs to go to the barn, Ma and Grandma were in the kitchen, and I smelled the coffee.

"Mornin', Delia," said Grandma. The set of her face did not match her greeting, and I suspected my pa would be hearing harsh words from his own ma shortly. She'd probably drag him out of bed, where I suspected he was resting.

My friend Rosa came down with the measles, and her mother would not allow us to see each other while she was bound to her room with a fever. The word *fever* brought a chill to my bones, for too often it had brought fear and sorrow to our family. Nevertheless, Rosa's quarantine came too late, because it was not long before I found red splotches on my stomach and my own temperature rose.

Measles was a childhood illness that was known to bring some children to death's door, but Grandma did not seem worried. She bathed me in meal to ease the itching, and Ma quarantined me to my room, easing my fever with wet rags as I'd seen her do with Pa when he was ill. Emily, however, soon joined me in the quarantine. My fever broke in only two days, and though Grandma kept bathing me, my spots remained another week.

I worried about Rosa, but Ma learned at the church that Rosa was well again. Yet, Emily's fever persisted. After a week her rash became sores and her fever held tight, which only sent me to my knees with prayers to God, asking that

He be real and that He hear me. I begged Him not to take another sister. It was two more days before He answered my prayers, and Emily was awake and giggling like the gigglemug that she was.

Let me assure you that I did not neglect my devotions, and a prayer of gratitude was spoken that night. I must admit that at first, when I was allowed to return to my room and snuggled into my soft bed, I had been remiss in evening prayers, before remembering to kneel and tell God of my happiness. It was wrong to only ask God for things. Gratefulness and praise were requisite as well.

"What are you doing out of bed, Fidelia?" asked Emily, resting in her own fresh-laundered bedding.

"Thanking God that you are well, Em," I said, and my sister smiled and was lost to dreams before I said amen.

However, what surprised me most was the following evening, when I walked into Ma's room looking for her, and my eyes saw Pa on his knees beside the bed. I tiptoed out of the room, hoping he'd not seen me. For all his bantering and denial of the Almighty, my heart swelled that he was not fallen and damned to hell, and deep inside, I was sad that Ma had not seen this most unexpected sight.

Chapter 21

At the imminence of losing my only remaining sister, I resolved to be kinder, remembering my past efforts to escape to Rosa's home alone, without Emily. I began inviting Emily to the Brandt farm when I visited Rosa, and at home, we would sneak upstairs, just the two of us, after our evening meals, to read Old Testament tales together by the Betty lamp in our room. Emily would often chuckle as I read the odd names in the Bible. My sister's laughter was always contagious and lifted my spirits.

With this new resolve of mine, and with our good fortune, I decided I would confront Pa about how he'd changed, about how much we all missed him, the way he used to be. With his mood, I knew this was a brave endeavor. As much as Emily and I missed Pa's old playfulness, it pained me even more knowing Ma was filled with sadness because of Pa's ire.

It was a few days before Pa walked into the barn one morning when I had just finished filling a bucket with milk.

"Pa?"

"What is it?" he responded.

I walked near to him as he filled a bucket with feed for the horses and our one remaining ox.

"Remember back in Indiana, when you would play games with me and Emily, when you laughed with Mama? I loved those times. I don't want to see you so sad all the time."

Pa looked at me for a moment, staring, then returned to his task.

"Things were different in Indiana," he said as he worked. "We were happy there. The farm fed us and here we struggle for so little. Don't know why Father ever brought us here, Fidelia."

He poured the feed in the troughs, and I followed him from one stall to another.

"I know, Pa, but Ma is so sad, and Em and I . . . we love you, Pa."

Pa tossed the empty bucket back near the feed barrels, and I watched it roll until it was stopped by a hay bale.

"I love you too, daughter," uttered Pa in a grim voice as he walked out, just as Jeremy came into the barn.

"What did you do, Fidelia? John looks like the world had crushed him," said Jeremy, looking down at my startled face. "Well, I must say," my uncle continued before I could answer his question, "he does often look that way, doesn't he?"

Jeremy walked into his workshop, but I just stood where I'd been. I was surprised by those last words Pa had said as he left the barn, words I never recalled him saying to me before, though it sounded as if the words pained him. My whole being wanted to run after him, to wrap my arms about him, yet I knew in my mind that I had changed nothing. Pa had not laughed or smiled or blessed me with any glimmer of faith that our lives could change. He had not talked with me about what I said to him, about how we could be happy again, but why would he? That was but pure whimsy, because my pa did not have conversations with me. What worried me most was that he never talked with Ma, who seldom smiled now and spent her days set about her chores or lying in bed. I carried the bucket of milk into the house and handed it to Grandma. I had no idea what to do next, so I walked back out to the barn and into the workshop.

Jeremy had developed into quite the craftsman, building furnishings we needed in the house and often designing pieces for members at our church. They always paid him what they could afford, and much to Grandma's dismay, he often spent his earnings at the saloon in Austin or near the new stagecoach inn in Brushy town, often gallivanting with his older brother.

"What are ya building, Uncle Jeremy?" I asked.

He pulled two legs for a small table from the workbench, legs already tapered, and he laid them on the surface before him before he grabbed the spoke shave, running it down the length of a table leg, forming a curve to the wood.

"An eatin' table, for the Harrell family," he replied.

"Would I have to pay ya to build something for me?"

"No, Fidelia. What do you want?"

"A swing. A big swing for me and Em."

"That's easy. Which tree do ya want it hung on?"

"Oh . . . the big oak on the path to the trail."

"Anything for my favorite niece. You'll have one by tomorrow," said Jeremy with the enthusiasm held in his joy of creating new things.

As I went to gather eggs for Mama, I had an idea and ran back to the workshop.

"No, Uncle Jeremy. I want a big swing in the barn, from the tall rafters over where the hay bales sit. So, rain or shine, we can swing and sing to the horses. A swing big enough for both me and Emily."

Jeremy stared at me, then shook his head and grinned. "I might have to get permission for that one. But I believe it to be a grand idea," he said.

When I walked in the barn the next morning to milk the cows, there hung the prettiest swing I ever saw, falling from the high rafters, the seat wide enough for two sisters. My uncle had put a hook on the wall so that the swing could be fastened out of the way by a loop in the rope. Later that afternoon, I saw two swings also adorning the big oak on the path, and before supper, Em and I had tested them all.

After supper, after kitchen chores, and once the sun was falling in the west, I went and grabbed Mama's hand.

"Come, Mama," I said. I pulled her outside toward the barn. "Look. It's the swing Uncle Jeremy built for me. And I want you to swing on it while the last of the sunlight still shines through. Come. Sit here."

She resisted. Said she was tired, but I persisted until she smiled, sat down on the big swing, and pushed off with her feet as I sat down on a hay bale.

"I've never seen a swing inside a barn before today," said Ma.

Back and forth she went, not too high but with the steadiness of a rhythm only she knew. I watched her and heard the finches outside sing to each other.

Just before the last sunrays vanished, Ma came to a stop and got off the swing, brushing her blue cotton skirt down over her crinoline.

"I love you, Fidelia," she said, and smiled at me. "And we need to thank your uncle for his gift." I took my ma's hand as we walked back to the house.

In the morning, after I milked the cow, I sat on the swing and pushed myself as high as I could go, and then jumped off when I heard Pa coming. I grabbed the basket filled with fresh eggs and ran to help Ma and Grandma in the kitchen.

"Your ma doesn't feel well this morning, Delia," said Grandma. "She's still in bed, but I do thank you for helping me in the kitchen. Here, you knead this dough for our biscuits while I put some pork on the stove."

I put the cloth on the bread table, followed by the dough, and began to knead, wondering what was wrong with Ma. This was the third morning she had missed breakfast in the last week. Ma had seemed so happy last night in the barn. Em ran into the kitchen and helped get the plates and forks, and put some jam on the table.

"Ma is still in bed," she said to me.

"I know. Grandma told me," I said.

It was just at that moment that the door opened, and Pa walked into the room, his clothes disheveled and smelling of whiskey.

"It is nice of you to join your family for breakfast, son," said Grandma as she scowled at my pa. He said nothing and walked on to his room. We all worked quietly in the kitchen, listening intently to see if there would be a row when Ma saw Pa come in, but we heard nothing. Only silence in the house.

There was not much conversation at breakfast, but Grandpa waxed on about the swings Jeremy had sanded and hung for us.

"I believe I might try that swing out, the one hanging in

the barn. I've never had a swing in my barn before," said Grandpa, winking at me and Emily, and my sister, true to form, could not stop laughing.

"It'll hold me, right, Jeremy?" asked Grandpa.

"You bet, sir. Might even hold one of those horses."

With that, Emily could no longer contain herself and laughed so hard she almost slipped out of her chair.

CHAPTER 23

The year was 1850 and spring was upon us, another growing season. I was now ten; Emily, eight. The success of the farm was our focus, and I worked with Ma to get the vegetable garden planted. We planted sprouts from tomato seeds that Grandma had started, and then we added rows of squash, cucumber, and pepper seeds. Ma had asked to plant some beets, thinking how she could boil them and dye wools and cottons into reds and pinks. Early spring rains helped the garden flourish as the men planted fields of corn and onions. Grandpa finally decided to put in more cotton, saying it was a damned nuisance, but it was the moneymaker.

"I'm going over to Rosa's, Ma," I said on a sun-filled Monday afternoon. "All of my chores are done until supper this evening."

"All right, Fidelia. Don't be late getting home," she answered as she took the laundry from the clothesline.

"Em is reading by the tree."

"She didn't want to go with you?" asked Ma.

"No, not today," I said, and before Ma could say more, I took off through the trees.

No one was in the fields when I walked toward the house, which was strange on such a beautiful day. Rosa opened the door, her mouth drawn into a frown, a face I'd never seen on my friend.

"Fidelia, this will make you sad, but Abby died on Sunday night," she said. "Mama's out there now, helping Reka prepare her for burial."

I was not surprised by this news because I knew how feeble my old friend was, but sadness still filled me. That I would never again see her face, lined with history, nor hear her sweet voice, kind words, weighed heavy.

"Mama did so love Abby," said Rosa, and I followed her into the kitchen. "I've cut some flowers from the garden, and some wildflowers that fill the meadow where Abby used to sit. See. Let me trim the stems, and we'll go out to the cabin."

I sat down and watched Rosa trim the flowers, arrange them, and tie five arrangements with narrow hemp cords. She handed a bouquet to me.

"Let's go," she said.

I followed her, thinking the whole way how fortunate it was that I had come to visit Rosa when I did. I wanted to be here, but no one had come to tell us. I know she was just a slave, that the world considered her of no worth, but I would have been heartbroken had she been sent home to her daughter without me present.

I watched as Missus Brandt, outside the slave cabin, adjusted the collar of Abby's dress and brushed the gray hair back from her face with such tenderness, as my old friend lay in a pine box. I saw the shawl I had made wrapped about the woman's shoulders, and the sight filled me with a warmth like a hearth fire lit in winter.

"Oh, Fidelia, I hope you are not distressed that your shawl is buried with Abby," Missus Brandt said to me.

"No. No, Missus Brandt. I am honored. She's wrapped

in love. From all of us," I replied. Missus Brandt put her hand on my shoulder and pulled me close.

The men nailed the top of the coffin and lifted it—just the two of them, for old Abby was merely a whisper, a feather in the wind. The small graveyard behind the cabins was unkempt yet peppered with wildflowers, blue and orange, and the familiar open pit sat ready for the old woman. I stood there in my blue calico dress, my hair braided down my back, standing fixed as if I were part of the family, for in my heart I knew that I was. Missus Brandt said prayers, one in Spanish, and crossed herself. Abe's tears fell quietly, but there was no outcry, no weeping, for we all knew Abby had looked forward to this passage and to seeing her daughter again. She was tired and wanted eternal respite.

The sun shone down, warming us in spring's breeze. We waited as the men filled the grave, pounding down the dirt, putting some large rocks on top and hammering into the fresh soil a wooden cross. It was then that Rosa and I placed our flowers 'neath the cross. I wanted to hug Abby again, but that time had passed, yet I would never forget her warm embraces and her quiet spirit. Just the thought of her now, after all our visits in the field, after my readings to her, fills me with a calm gratitude. Her frailty had been so filled with fortitude, like the force of a meager ant, and her vast spirit had always permeated the sky around all of us.

Missus Brandt fixed our dinner, and I sat with the family, even Rosa's father, who had missed Abby's burial, and we ate amidst quiet conversation as if we were sitting in the pews of a church. It would not be a day for play, but I could not help but wonder how Abe felt out in the field, now at work, without the watchful gaze of his grandmother.

When I walked in the house, just in time to help Grandma with the supper meal, I told her about Abby. About how Missus Brandt wanted the old woman and the men freed, how Abby loved the new sun of each dawn, how much she wanted to see her own daughter in heaven.

"Is she the one you stitched that beautiful shawl for, Delia?"

"Yes, Grandma, and guess what? She was wrapped in it, inside her coffin," I told her.

"Oh my. Such a loss of your beautiful work." She looked softly at me. "But I do understand, if she was so beloved."

"I was elated, Grandma," I said. "Like a piece of me would embrace my friend for eternity. Where's Ma?"

"I think she is in her room, dear."

I walked into Ma's room and saw her take a drink from the bottle the doctor had given her for Emily's fevers. *Was Ma sick?* I remembered the mornings she had missed breakfast, feeling unwell.

"Ma?"

"Yes, dear?" she replied. She slipped the bottle into a drawer.

"My friend Abby died."

Ma looked confused, but then remembered. "She was your friend, the old woman at the Brandt farm?"

"Yes, Ma. We buried her today, right there on their farm."

"Oh, dear. I'm sorry, Fidelia. I must go over to visit

Missus Brandt one day soon." She sat down on the side of her bed. "I am tired and think I shall take a nap. Will you tell Grandma, dear?"

"Yes, ma'am. Are you sick?" I asked.

"No, dear. I just need a bit more sleep," said Ma, her voice weak.

"I love you, Ma." I closed the door gently as I returned to the kitchen.

The supper meal was not well attended. Ma was napping, and Uncle Jeremy and Pa were absent, which was an oft-occurring event. Emily and I talked with Grandma and Grandpa about Abby and the Brandt farm, about the crops that had been planted, and about the recent pieces of furniture that Uncle Jeremy had built; we warily avoided the topic of the empty chairs at the table.

I saw Rosa and her ma when we went to worship services on Sunday, but I knew that the summertime would have me and Em working harder than ever as the men tended to the crops. It turned out to be a hot summer with rain a rarity, but Grandpa managed to eke out a satisfactory harvest as Emily and I resumed classes with Ma in the fall. Ma gave us our assignments, asked us questions, but the distant look in her eyes did not escape my notice. Emily, on the other hand, was always in a daydream or playing with the animals or with Bear, and she seemed unaware of the changes in our family, changes that kept me awake at night after prayers, before sleep carried me to my dreams.

CHAPTER 24

With the harvest almost done, I found more time to run over to the Brandt farm, sometimes with Emily in tow. Rosa and I could talk for hours, about everything: our lessons, the other children at our church, even the fears I would sometimes reveal. Rosa would console me, assure me that all would be well, for my friend seemed to have no fears of her own, only the isolation she sometimes felt by being an only child, what with her brother being older and gone. Emily would talk about her fear of snakes, of which we'd seen a few on our farm, including a rattlesnake last year. At the slightest movement in tall grass, Emily would run screaming. We would lift each other up when sad, and most of the time, laughter came easy to us—even Emily, of course. Emily loved the Brandt goats, their playfulness, and wanted to take one home, but Grandpa had no need for goats.

As harvest came to an end, Grandpa decided I should learn how to shoot a rifle. Me, a girl!

"Women in Texas are hard as nails when it comes to defending their families, their land," he said. "With some renegade Indians attacking farms up around Lampasas, I think you and your ma need to know how to shoot. Go get your ma, Fidelia."

When Ma came out to join us, she was drying her hands

on her apron, looking flustered. "Father, why do I need to learn to shoot?" she asked. "We have enough men around here."

"Mariah, we are close enough to neighbors, to the city, that I don't expect trouble. But if the menfolk are gone or are out in the fields, I want you to be able to defend yourself. There's always that old Newton shotgun hanging by the fireplace."

Ma scowled but joined in the practice behind the barn. Within a week I was a sharpshooter, better than my mother. Well, maybe I wasn't quite a sharpshooter, but I hit a few targets. Ma's heart was not in the learning, but I wanted to be as good as Pa and Uncle Jeremy, so my uncle spent afternoons practicing with me, showing me how to sight my target and how to adjust for the kickback. He taught me how to load the powder in the shotgun and how to clean the barrel. Within a month, I showed Grandpa how I could load, aim, and hit the straw man he'd nailed onto a tree trunk at the far end of the cornfield. I was filled with a new confidence. I stood taller, or so I thought.

"Well, girl, I might be sending you out to hunt supper next time. Bring us back some quail for a fine meal," said Grandpa. We all laughed, even Ma.

As the threat of winter loomed, Rosa and I sat in her barn one day and I told her all about learning to shoot, and she was in wonder of me.

"I don't think my papa would ever permit me to do that," Rosa said. "Mama, either. Though I did see her shoot a handgun, a pepperbox she carries in her leather pouch, once when we were out riding and a snake startled the horses. She shot at it, but the snake slithered away too fast for her to kill it. I think the gunshot scared the horse more than the snake."

"Oh, Rosa, I wish we could go riding together," I said. "I don't have a horse of my own. But we wouldn't have a gun to shoot snakes."

"Maybe my mama will take us both out one day. I'll ask her."

Excitement welled up inside me at the thought of riding through the countryside, just like the men. I decided to ask Uncle Jeremy to show me how to ride a horse so that I wouldn't appear so clumsy riding at the Brandt farm.

It turned out to be a chilly day when Uncle Jeremy saddled up a horse for me. I tied a warm shawl about my shoulders to keep me warm, and my uncle lifted me up.

"Don't I need to learn how to get up myself?" I asked.

"Yes, you do. We'll work on that after a short ride. And you need to learn how to properly saddle a horse."

Emily watched, laughing at my clumsiness, from the back porch as I followed Uncle Jeremy down the path toward the trail. I felt so grown up, though only ten years old, almost eleven. Here I was, riding this horse down the trail, and I knew how to shoot a rifle. I was not the little girl I had been in Indiana.

Ma continued to miss breakfasts and I'd see her eyes glazed over. She'd tell me she was tired, but I prayed at night that she was well. However, I managed to arrange a visit to the Brandt farm for Ma, so we bundled up on a cold December day, the two of us plus Emily, and walked through the trees and along the field to the big farmhouse.

I had already told Missus Brandt that I wanted her to

show Ma how to make her chocolate drink. I carried a custard pie Grandma had baked for Missus Brandt. Just as we cleared the trees, Ma bent over as if in pain and vomited into the brush.

"Ma," I said, and carefully handed the pie to my sister. "Ma, are you not well?"

I pulled the handkerchief from Ma's dress pocket and handed it to her. She wiped her face, then the hem of her dress.

"Oh, Fidelia. I cannot go," she said. "I'm not well enough, child. And look at me, a mess. Please beg Missus Brandt's forgiveness. I must go home."

"Ma, you will not go home alone." I turned to Emily. "Em, with careful steps you take the pie over to Missus Brandt and tell her our ma is sick. Tell her we will schedule for another day."

"I will," said Emily.

"You come right back home, Em," I said, and put my arm around Ma's waist, heading back the way we'd come.

Grandma ran to us when I helped Ma into the kitchen. Ma's face was almost gray.

"Oh, dear. What happened?" Grandma asked.

"Ma got sick on the way to the neighbor's farm. She heaved," I said.

"I'm just tired. I need to lie down," said Ma, walking toward her room.

"Daughter, you need to stop sipping that laudanum. It's changed you, made you sick," said Grandma.

Ma said nothing, but tiptoed to her bedroom, and I went to fill a pitcher with water for her bedside. I did not understand why Ma was drinking the medicine if she didn't need it. Plainly, God had not been answering my prayers.

The following week we walked again to visit Missus Brandt. Ma had eaten a good breakfast and seemed better, though we carried no offering of pie or cake on this visit. Emily ran straight out to the barn to see the goats, and Missus Brandt had a colorful table set for dinner, including some *champurrado*.

"Mariah, your daughter has asked that I show you how I make my *champurrado*," Missus Brandt said. "After we have eaten, we shall sit in the kitchen and make a pot of chocolate while we visit. I apologize for my husband's absence, but he has traveled into Austin on some political matter."

"You are so gracious to have invited me back and prepared such a fine meal," Ma said. "I am certain the whole of my family will be happy if I learn to make this chocolate drink Fidelia has spoken of so often."

"It is such a pleasure to have your girls visit, especially for Rosa, who is the only child at the farm now, the only daughter. Your Fidelia is like part of our family here and was most kind to Abby. You know, it was Abby who delivered me of my baby girl. There was no time for a doctor, and Abby had more experience midwifing than any doctor."

"I wish I had met her. Fidelia was always talking about Abby, like she had an extra grandmother looking out after her."

Missus Brandt nodded and smiled. "Fidelia has wanted to go riding with me and Rosa, but I would want your permission first," said Missus Brandt. "May she ride with us one day?"

"Well, Fidelia doesn't know . . ." started Ma.

"Ma, Uncle Jeremy has taught me to ride the chestnut mare at our farm," I said.

"Well, I had no idea. You should have told me, Fidelia." Ma turned back to Missus Brandt. "I will check with my brother-in-law to make sure Fidelia has the skills, and if so, then yes, she may ride with you. I know how much she enjoys her friendship with your Rosa."

Rosa and I walked outside, leaving Ma and Missus Brandt to visit. I looked across the meadow, toward the big trees, for the old woman in the hickory chair and found the horizon empty of my old friend. Rosa and I walked out to the barn to look at the horses.

"This one, the dappled mare, is mine," said Rosa as she brushed the horse's nose. "The black stallion over there," she pointed behind us, "is Mama's horse."

"Which one will I ride?" I asked.

"Hmmm, let us look," Rosa said, and walked along the stalls. "How about this one? The gelded pinto. He is quite gentle."

The horse came toward us and put his nose over the stall gate, and I slowly put my hand near his face so he could smell me. When he nuzzled my hand, I stroked him.

"What's his name?" I asked.

"I don't remember. We'll ask Abe," said Rosa.

We sat on the bench just outside the barn door, and I felt a breeze, a chilled gust of December.

"Christmas is next week. I suppose we'll see each other at church, yes?" I asked.

"I am certain. We'll sing carols and light candles. I love

the carols. Tonight, Pa is bringing our tree and we will decorate it. Do you have one?" asked Rosa.

"No. Pa won't allow no tree in our house. But if the pastor brings one over, as he has before, we will put it in the barn, or near the porch, and Em and I will decorate it. Hey, can you come over one day? We have a grand new swing in our barn."

"A swing? Inside the barn?"

"Yes, Uncle Jeremy made it for us," I answered.

"Your uncle is very cute. Does he have a girlfriend?"

"Not that I know of," I said, wondering what Rosa was thinking. My uncle was so much older than the two of us, but then I thought of her ma and how young she looked compared to Rosa's father. Boys had not crossed my mind, except that I had little in common with them.

"Rosa, I wish you had met Aunt Audrey. She was only eighteen when she died, when we first came here, but I've never told you the story of how she'd run away with a French fur trapper on our journey to Texas."

Rosa perked up at my words. "A fur trapper?" she asked.

"She loved him, and he loved her, but then she died from the fever, so young."

"What a tragedy, Fidelia," said Rosa, her eyes watering.

"It was a tragedy, Rosa. Audrey was beautiful and so filled with life, and I believe God was quite cruel to take her. Sometimes I wish my pa had never found her in the forest and brought her back to us."

Rosa just looked at me, her eyes filled with both curiosity and dismay.

"She ran off with the trapper and his Indian, and my pa had to go looking for her. Her beloved—his name was

Edmund—later came to Texas looking for her. He wanted to marry Aunt Audrey, but she had already died. He was terribly distraught."

Gloom filled me when I thought of my aunt's early death, as I recounted the events to my friend. A sadness whirled about the two of us and swiftly vanished when Abe walked up to the barn.

"G'day, girls," he said.

"Abe," said Rosa, "what is the name of that pinto in the barn?"

"That is Pedro."

"Pedro . . . that will be your horse, Fidelia," said my friend as if she ruled the entire kingdom. And I believe she did. My best friend, the queen of the Brandt farm.

Chapter 25

When spring came in March, Pastor Wieland told the congregation that there would be a picnic near Brushy Creek and welcomed all to partake. Ma said she'd bring beans. Grandma pledged to bring a cherry pie and a batch of cornbread, and Missus Wieland, a young woman the pastor had married last year, said she would arrange for games for the children. Rosa, Emily, and I were eager for the day to arrive at the end of the month.

We were all busy with the planting season, yet daily Emily and I had our lessons with Ma just before dinner. One day, all my chores were done when I gathered my reader at my bedside and sat at the dining table, telling my sister to get her tablet. I read a couple of pages, but Ma still had not arrived.

"Where is she?" I asked Emily.

"Don't know."

Grandma was out planting in the vegetable garden, but Ma was not with her, so I went to Ma's room. She lay on her bed, asleep.

"Ma?" I asked.

There was no response, so I shook her shoulder.

"Ma, wake up. Em and I are waiting for our lesson."

Ma did not answer, so I shook her harder, and with a sudden fright, I saw something was wrong. Her arms were limp, and she would not wake. I prayed she was not dead.

I ran to the garden.

"Grandma, something's wrong with Ma. I cannot wake her," I said.

Grandma dropped her spade and yanked off her gloves, dropping them and running into the house with me. She was unable to wake Ma and looked distressed.

"Is she dead, Grandma?" I asked.

"No, dear. She's not, but she's not well. Go fill a small bowl or pitcher with water and bring it to me. Quick," said Grandma. I ran to the kitchen, then to the well. Grandma took the bowl and poured the water on my ma's face. I gasped. Ma stirred, seeming unaware of where she was.

"Enough of this, daughter! Enough!" said Grandma, pulling open the drawers of Ma's dressing table. She pulled out the amber-colored bottle, the one with the medicine, and walked out of the room as Ma sat up in bed.

I did not know what to do, so I followed Grandma outside. With the full force of her extended arm, she struck the bottle against the corner of the house so that it shattered in pieces and the liquid splashed to the ground.

The bottle Grandma carried was the medicine I'd seen Ma drinking on occasion, and now Grandma was angry. This did not happen often, but when it did, things were about to happen. When Grandma took charge like this, people listened, and I wished with all my might that this was a trait Grandma had passed on to me. I followed her back inside to Ma's bedroom.

"Mariah, you will not destroy yourself, not because of a man, even if he is my son, and not with these two little girls looking up to you as an example. There will be no more laudanum in this house," Grandma said.

Ma sat on the bed, her feet on the floor. She still seemed

ET THE LITTLE BIRDS SING

began to cry.

"I know what the problem is, girl. I know my son is
being a fool and neglecting his duties to his family, but just
as I expect more of him, I expect more out of you. And have
no doubt that I will deal with John. Now get yourself
together, dry your face, and sit with your girls' lessons.
They know what to do, but you will be present."

Grandma turned to leave, then faced us. "I will make a
pot of coffee. Fidelia, go sit at the table with your sister.
Give your ma a few moments."

I followed Grandma into the kitchen and sat next to
Emily. Thoughts spun in my head as Emily looked at me for
answers, having heard all the commotion.

"Ma was sick," I whispered to her.

I felt so filled with glee that Ma was not dead, as I'd first
believed. I did not understand how the medicine was
making her sick, but I knew that now was not the time to
ask questions. It came clear to me that whatever was
happening was connected to Ma's sadness and loneliness,
and my pa, at least in my own eyes, was to blame. *What
was Grandma going to do about it?*

Ma came to the table just as Grandma set a cup of
steaming creamed coffee in front of her.

"Do you girls want a drink of milk?" asked Grandma.

"No, thank you, ma'am," I answered for the both of us.

Ma smiled at us, then took a slow sip of her coffee. "I
apologize, girls, for being absent. I am feeling better now,"
she said.

I started reading aloud from my lesson. Emily just
listened, and Ma was present, but her mind was plainly not
with us or the words I read.

I never knew what happened between Pa and his mother, but I must tell you that when the church picnic came around, Pa went with us. I could not have been more surprised, and Ma had to introduce him to many of our church friends who had never met him.

"I am so pleased you could join us today, John," said Jacob Wieland. "I know planting season is a difficult time to get away."

Pa nodded but did not smile. I knew he felt awkward being there with all these people he considered strangers, but he was pleasant enough and did engage in some conversations with some cotton farmers. I was glad that he came, and Ma wore a new rosy pink on her cheeks, a sign of her well-being.

Emily, Rosa, and I ran down to play near the creek, trying to catch some tadpoles in a yellow bowl now empty of Ma's baked beans. When we were finished playing, our hems muddied, we walked back to where Grandma had spread a large quilt. I saw Ma sitting alone, crying. Confused, I looked about only to see Pa walking away in the distance, his head bent down toward the trail that led to our farm.

"Ma, what is wrong?" I asked.

"Oh, dear, your pa was not happy with me and decided to go home." She brushed her eyes with her hand, tried to compose herself. "We are fine. Your pa just had some work to do at the barn."

I hugged Ma as Emily and Rosa looked on, Rosa's eyes wide. Grandma walked toward us, and I saw Grandpa and Jeremy across the way with the pastor.

"Dear, where did John go? I saw him walking across the

field," said Grandma.

"He's gone home," said Ma. I could see Ma wanted to say more, but clearly would not when we were present. In my head my thoughts ran wild: *Was he angry Grandma made him come, had he been offended by our pastor's greeting, was he mad at Ma for her drinking the medicine?*

I wanted to know what had happened, but there was little chance of that. Neither Grandma nor Ma would reveal such details to me, but I'm certain Grandma would be querying Pa at home in my absence.

"You girls need to go down to the stream and wet your hems and rub out the dirt, then come back right away so as not to get muddied again. Pastor Wieland is going to cut some watermelon and the cake in a few minutes, so hurry back," said Grandma.

We walked slowly and in silence back to the creek.

"What happened with your ma?" asked Rosa.

"I don't know, but I know Pa does not like to socialize with the church, so I guess he went home," I replied, feeling embarrassed. Emily looked at me, her eyes filled with questions not uttered. Though Emily was filled with happiness most of the time, she was uncomfortable when confused.

Suddenly, I knew what I'd do. I would ask Pa what happened. Tomorrow morning, in the barn. He'd likely get irritated, but I would persist, for I knew Pa always spilled his feelings when he was angry.

The last of the cow's warm milk dripped into the bucket and some of it inched down my arm when I looked up to see Pa walk into the barn and begin breaking open a hay bale.

"Pa, can I ask you something?" I asked.

"Don't know how I can stop ya."

"Why was Ma crying yesterday? At the picnic," I asked.

He glared at me, just as I'd expected he would. "You mind your own business, girl. Take that bucket into the kitchen. Your grandma is waiting on it."

"But, Pa. Ma had been so happy yesterday . . . glad that you'd come to the picnic. Then she was crying, and you left."

"Enough, girl! Your ma's making herself useless with drinking that medicine or whatever it is. There's enough trouble here. We don't need no more."

Pa rammed the pitchfork hard into the hay bale, and I knew it was time to say no more. I grabbed the handle of the bucket and headed for the house. I'd get the eggs after a bit.

CHAPTER 26

That night, at our supper, Jeremy and Pa were missing. Ma said they went to Georgetown, and Grandma did not look happy. I was hoping Grandpa would come up with one of his stories to break the silence at the table. And sure enough, he did.

"You know, back at the fort in Indiana, when I was still a young man, about eighteen, there were plenty of brawls," he said. "Got into a couple myself, when my judgment faltered. I remember once these two fellas got into an argument over a woman at the fort, a woman of less than proper repute."

Grandma glared at Grandpa, and I saw him nod at her.

"She was a beauty, as I recall," continued Grandpa. "But these two fellas were going at it pretty good. The big one giving the other scoundrel a pounding, and when I started fearing for the fella's own life, I decided I'd be the one to stop it."

"What happened, Father?" asked Ma. "And the woman, where did she go?"

"Well, women like that didn't go anywhere. She stayed at the fort, started working in the kitchen. But me, I got a black eye and a swollen jaw, yet we managed to get the big fella outside and onto his horse. He was just drunk and bruised enough to let his horse carry him home.

"That little fella, he got the best of the night. Miss Betsy,

161

the woman they were fighting over, nursed his wounds for almost a week and they'd wink at each other across the dining hall. Never knew what happened to the two of them."

"Do you think that's what happened to Pa and Jeremy, Grandpa? They're at the saloon, maybe fighting?" I asked.

"No telling, Fidelia. Between John's temper and Jeremy being short on prudence, wouldn't surprise me."

The room fell quiet again. In the morning Uncle Jeremy and Pa were nowhere to be found, and Grandpa, normally the most easygoing man I'd known, was fuming. It was planting season, and after he fed the livestock, he hooked up his plow to the old ox and headed to the cotton field. The cotton had to be planted. He worked until dark, coming in for a late supper, saying nothing as he ate, and then he was straight to bed. There'd been no word of my pa or my uncle.

For two more days Grandpa worked himself to the bone, each day till the sun had left us. During that time, my ma had gone out to the field and helped her father-in-law, throwing in the seed as the lines were tilled. On that second day, after she came in before suppertime, I walked with her to the pond, where she stripped down to her bloomers and waded into the waters, washing herself clean. I truly did want to join her in the cool spring waters, but I allowed her the time I knew she needed. She floated in the shaded part of the pond and rubbed the soil and sweat of the day off with an ease I had not seen in my ma for a long time. Watching her stilled the jitters through my whole body, and I leaned back on the tree, where sleep tried to capture me until Bear's fur ticked my ankle. When she walked out of the water, she donned the clean cotton frock I'd brought for her. I carried Ma's soiled dress and stockings as we walked back to the house, where we helped Grandma prepare a meal for so few of us.

Just as we began clearing the plates from the table, the door opened and in walked Pa and Jeremy.

"Well, sons, it is thoughtful of you both to show up now that the cotton is planted," said Grandpa with a glare that could have pierced like a sword.

Jeremy went straight up the stairs without a word to anyone.

"Mother, is there any grub left? I am mighty hungry," said Pa.

"Me too," said Jeremy, coming back down the stairs with a clean shirt.

"Pa, I am sorry we weren't here to help you with the planting. Jeremy got himself locked up, and I didn't want to leave him there. We went down to the Spicer Tavern the other night, and Jeremy got into a game of Faro with Seth and some other men. I was surprised to see Seth still in these parts, and I was drinking at the bar, conversing, when I heard the gunshot."

"A gunshot?" said Grandma. "Is Jeremy injured?"

"Wasn't him that got injured, Mother. It was him that drew his pistol. He told me the other guy was cheating, and when they exchanged heated words, the fighting escalated. My brother thought a bullet would resolve the matter and shot at the guy."

"Oh, my Lord!" said Grandma.

"Can't be too bad if they let him out of jail," said Grandpa, his wide eyes and his eyebrows raised, awaiting validation.

"Well, he was lucky the bullet only grazed the fellow's leg," said Pa. "I convinced the scoundrel to drop the charges, and the sheriff let Jeremy go with the proviso that he is never to enter the tavern again."

"Well, that may be a good thing," said Grandma. "Maybe you should take his gun away, William."

"I will give that some thought over time. This is not a land to wander around unarmed. Especially if you're gambling," replied Grandpa. He glared at his sons, his displeasure plain. "And I'm talking to both of you."

"I'll fix you both a plate of what's left," said my ma to her sons. "And I'll bring a basin of fresh water for you two to wash up."

I saw a weak smile pass between Ma and Pa, making me feel a brief assurance of better times, though I was old enough to know that seeing him smile and avert his eyes to the floor more likely revealed his shame. Of exactly what, I was not sure.

The next morning, after breakfast, Grandpa sent his sons out to the fields to plant the beans, but he did not follow them.

"Hey, Fidelia, go get your fishing pole," Grandpa said.

"Yes, Grandpa," I responded, my heart full of glee.

"Run in and tell your ma that you and I are going fishin'."

When I returned, he pulled me up behind him on his horse, which meant we were going to the river. We'd surely come home with a basket full of bounty for supper—with luck, a couple of shiny bass. It would be a good day.

CHAPTER 27

Emily and I still did our readings through the summer, but other lessons would wait for the fall, after the crops were harvested. I would read verses of the Bible to my sister and she would read from our reader. There were days that I wished I had kept Audrey's book of poems.

Now that Emily was almost ten years old, she helped me with the vegetable garden. We both had stitching to do a few days each week, and I continued to milk the cows and fed the chickens. Emily helped Ma churn the butter and was learning how to make candles. Though we used kerosene more than candles, Grandma could sell candles at the market. Emily and I cherished our time together, but she had developed a love for helping Grandma in the kitchen. Over time, Emily's baked breads exceeded the excellence of those made by Ma and Grandma, and we all teased her about how she would make some man a fine wife one day.

In spite of the chores, I still found time to visit the Brandt farm. When the terrible heat of August came, Rosa told me she was going down to Mexico in September to visit her grandparents and, on the way, to visit her father's brother in Tusculum, near the Cibola Creek. Places unfamiliar to me.

"I have never even met my uncle near the Cibola Creek, and I've only visited my grandparents once before," said Rosa. She could hardly contain her excitement, though she

SANDRA FOX MURPHY

said she dreaded the long journey in the wagon. "But we have weeks to play before we leave, Fidelia. Let's go riding. I'll ask Abe to saddle the horses."

"Isn't he out readying for the harvest?" I asked.

"Maybe. Let's go look in the barn."

"What about your ma? She needs to go with us," I said.

"Not really. We can ride. I do it all the time," said Rosa as we both ran toward the barn.

Abe was there, cleaning out the horse stalls. He helped Rosa and me saddle our horses.

"What about Missus Brandt? She's going, isn't she?" asked Abe.

"No, Abe. Just us girls. We won't go far. Just in the meadows by the cotton fields," replied Rosa. Abe raised his eyebrows.

Rosa effortlessly mounted her mare, and I hoisted myself somewhat awkwardly onto Pedro. Off we went, around the edge of the fields of cotton. In the distance I saw Abe watching us, and then he disappeared as Rosa led us into the trees, on toward the creek.

I had ridden Pedro once before, when we went riding up the trail with Missus Brandt on an easy and relaxing jaunt in the early evening. But I was not as experienced as Rosa, and she was moving faster than I could keep up.

"Wait, Rosa," I yelled, unsure if she'd heard me.

Finally, she looked back and slowed her horse's gait. We continued on, weaving around the large cedar brake and then through the trees toward the sound of running water.

"Won't your mama be mad at us, Rosa?" I asked. "For riding without her?"

"Yes, but only for a bit. She knows I can handle the

166

horses, but we shall have fun today, won't we?"

"I'm afraid she will worry for our well-being," I said, likely more to myself than Rosa. I was a girl who abided the rules, yet I loved my friend's free spirit and would likely follow her anywhere.

The water eased its way through the creek, even in the midst of August, dispelling a coolness and calm about us. The willows and cottonwoods shaded the path along the edge.

"Do you want to swim?" asked Rosa.

"Maybe," I answered warily. I was not sure it was a good idea, two girls alone. There could be snakes nearby, or scoundrels living off the land, like our old farmhand Seth. We approached an embankment where the trees stood tall when Rosa called out, "Look!"

"What?" I asked, startled at her cry and fearing trouble.

"There's a cave. Let's see how far it goes." She dismounted her horse, looking about for a strong branch to tie the reins. I just stared at the dark hole she had pointed toward. *How many risks were we going to take today?*

With both of our horses tethered, we tiptoed into the darkness. My foot slipped on the dampness, and my friend caught my elbow. I wished for a lantern, but we had no light—we made our way by running our hands along the dank rock walls, just dirt and rock. We had not gone far before a sliver of sunlight lit the small cave, a break in roots and rocks above us that merged two worlds. We felt like we were in a secret room.

"Look, Rosa—there, where the light hits the floor of the room," I said.

Moss glowed green in the dim, gray cave. It was cool where we stood, unlike the sultry day above us.

"Oh, Fidelia, this is our secret room. No one can find us here."

"Well, yes, they can. The horses are waiting by the tree," I answered.

Rosa rolled her eyes at me. "Next time we come, we shall bring a picnic," she said.

"Next time?"

Rosa stepped into a puddle. It was clear that the creek ran through the cave when the rains came. My nose filled with the fragrance of dirt, enhanced by its dankness.

"We are not supposed to be here. I think we should go," I said.

Rosa's mama was angry, just as I had feared, when we came into the house after delivering our horses to the barn. Abe had told her we'd gone riding alone. And just as my friend had expected, her riding privileges were taken away and her father said she would stay home and work on her embroidery and her Bible reading, which meant that, for two weeks, she and I could no longer play. Missus Brandt told me I could come back to the farm in exactly two weeks, but I feared there would be little time to visit my friend before her family left on their journey to Mexico.

Back home, I dreaded that my ma or pa would be told of Rosa's and my escapade, but no word was ever spoken of it, and I suspected that Rosa's mother knew our transgression was not my idea. Bear and I spent my rare free hours moping under the big oak tree near the house, but Emily always showed up to cheer me. One day she walked out with my muslin and threads and we sat and stitched until it was time to help in the kitchen.

When two weeks had passed, when my chores were

done and the men were beginning the harvest in the field, I ran towards the meadow by the Brandt farm. I did not know when they would leave for their visit to Rosa's grandparents.

Out of breath, I knocked on the Brandt's front door and was greeted by Rosa.

"Can I come in? Has your confinement ended?" I asked.

"Yes, but we cannot ride yet."

"But we can visit? Can we just go out and sit by the tree, over where Abby used to sit?"

"Let's. I'll go tell Mama," replied Rosa.

She returned in a moment and we walked out toward the empty cotton fields, where I saw Abe and three others weeding. The old oak blocked the afternoon sun, and we sat in the shade of the tree.

"I want to go back to the cave," said Rosa.

"Rosa, we can't. You will be punished again, and I may be banned from your farm forever. We cannot." My eyes fell on my friend's face, pleading. "And, besides, you are leaving soon for Mexico," I said. "I will miss you horribly."

"Oh, no, I'm not leaving. Papa has moved our trip. To spring."

I inhaled, long and slow. Relieved.

"Then we'll go again. But not now. I'm certain your mama's watching us. We shall wait. And we can walk there . . . it will just take longer."

Rosa smiled.

Gladness filled me. My friend would be here through the year. We would have good times together. We had both heard words spoken at church about a school being raised not far from our farms. Rosa and I would be together each day, reading and learning and staying best of friends.

CHAPTER 28

It was one of the first cool days of October when Rosa convinced her mama to let us take a picnic to the meadow. In spite of our eagerness to return to our secret room by the creek, my stomach lurched. I had never before lied to Missus Brandt, who had been so kind to me. I suppose I did not truly lie, for I only failed to reveal the truth. It troubled me to lie, always fearing that I might disappoint my grandparents.

"Here, girls, take this basket," Missus Brandt said. "I cooked some chicken and biscuits, and there is some blueberry jam and one mint for each of you. And a cloth to sit upon."

She handed the basket to Rosa, who thanked and hugged her. I watched, my tummy still queasy, and was amazed by the ease with which my friend deceived her mother.

I followed Rosa out the door, both of us wearing our cloaks, should a chill beset us. We walked slowly, with a purpose known only by us. We walked through the meadow, and I turned back to see if anyone stood watching. I saw no one, and we walked on through the trees and another long field until we came to the cedars and circumvented them to get to the meadows along the creek's edge, thick with foliage and the cover of tall trees. The leaves were still green, for the heat of summer had only recently left and the winter chills had not arrived. The water trickled through the creek, urging us on toward our destination.

Again, we did not have a lantern, but entered into the cave by feeling our way, as we had before. The light was not as bright as last time because of the season and clouded sky, but Rosa lifted the lid on the basket and spread the cloth on our floor of dirt and rock. It felt as if we had our own little home, a secret place for a gathering of friends.

We ate slowly, savoring the food Missus Brandt had prepared as well as our moments together, knowing that in a few months we would be separated for too long a time.

"Do you think your mama will take us riding one day, before winter sets in?" I asked Rosa.

"I think she will. She told me that she had missed our rides together, though on a couple occasions in September she went riding alone. Did you know that Samuel, the Bratton boy, tried to kiss me one day after church?"

"No. How bold of him," I responded in shock. Sometimes I forgot that we were at that age when we would soon be women, when our waists would narrow, our hips widen. Rosa's bosom was beginning to fill her bodice, but mine remained unchanged.

"Should I let him?" asked Rosa.

"I don't think so. Your reputation is more important than his eagerness, Rosa."

She looked disappointed.

"Besides, he will only brag about it to his friends," I added.

Rosa spread some jam on her biscuit.

"You are always so smart, Fidelia. And always a good friend. I so anticipate my first kiss, but I think your advice is practical, and I'll wait."

I pondered her words, suspicious of just how long she would wait. Not long, I imagined. I thought of my aunt and how Audrey was so sweet and generous, but reckless, just like my dear Rosa.

A snap of thunder startled us. Then we heard the tapping of rain on the ground above us. A storm had come in from the west, but we were safe and warm in our room.

"We'll have to walk home in the rain, Rosa," I said.

"Not yet. It will pass. These storms always pass quickly."

We talked of dresses and our embroidery, laughed about my discordant singing at church. As I took the first bite of mint, I noticed the hem of my dress was wet, and my shoes damp. I looked down and saw the water seeping across the cave's floor.

"We need to leave. Now!" I yelled at my friend, panic filling me.

"Oh, dear. We will be soaked when we get home. I hope Mama hasn't sent Abe looking for us," said Rosa.

We gathered everything into the basket, but the water was already up to our knees, dripping heartily into the room from the entrance as well as from the opening above and down the stone walls. We pushed our way through the heaviness of the water and into the darkness of the path to the opening, feeling our way with our arms extended.

The water continued rising as we struggled through the depths toward the light at the opening where the creek poured in, and my heart was racing. We had been foolish, lying to our parents, disregarding the dangers around us. *What if something happened to us? What if our parents found naught but our drenched and limp bodies at the side of the creek?* I pushed first through the water, stepping up on the rock to find the skies darkened and purging torrents of rain.

The creek ran strong and pulled me as I turned and grabbed my friend's free hand, pulling her toward me. I saw the terror on her face as the strength of the water held her. I tossed the picnic basket toward the tree and then leaned back, with both hands and all my weight, and Rosa rose from the cave. We both struggled, holding hands, in the rushing current. We had escaped the rage of the water as we climbed up the stream's banks, but would we escape the wrath of our parents?

When we reached the meadow, the sun was shining, and we strolled slowly. Slowly, so that the sunshine would dry our clothes. Slowly, so that our fear would subside and our hearts would stop pounding. I took Rosa's hand and held it as we walked. I held it until we reached the barn at the Brandt farm, our dresses still a bit damp.

"Oh, girls. Look at your hair. Did you get caught in the rain?" said Missus Brandt as we walked into the house.

"Yes, Mama. We sheltered under the trees. That's why we're so tardy. We ate every bit of the lunch you packed us. Thank you, Mama," said Rosa.

"Change your frock, Rosa, and pull out one of your dresses for Fidelia," said Missus Brandt, who took the basket and walked away to the kitchen.

Rosa hugged me. "Thank you, Fidelia. Thank you for saving us. What should I ever do without you?"

"You will never have to know. Come to my house later this week, and we can swing in the barn." I smiled. "Bring your embroidery and we can sit and work together for a bit."

After we had changed and after Rosa had braided my damp hair, I meandered home, thinking of our illicit picnic, our harrowing adventure, filled with gratitude that we were both unharmed and our deceit undiscovered.

Harvest season had passed. Grandpa said we'd had a good year, and when Christmas came, he led a horse out of the barn toward me as I sat daydreaming on the swing under the oak. Mama stood on the porch, watching, and Emily stood beside her wearing the yellow dress that I'd outgrown. After years of wear and laundry, that yellow fabric still brightened the view.

"Fidelia, merry Christmas," Grandpa said.

I looked at him and then at the unfamiliar horse, a grand chestnut bay.

"He's yours, Fidelia."

I looked at Grandpa, then towards Ma, who was smiling as she watched us.

"Mine?"

"Yours, girl! And you better take care of him." He handed me the reins.

"What's his name?" I asked.

"He's two years old, and his name is Trapper."

I directly thought of Edmund. Yes, Trapper was a good name.

"Do you think you can handle him? He is gentle. He rides easy."

"Can I take him for a ride? Now?"

"Yes, you can. For now, just around the trail, where I

can see you."

I hoisted myself up on Trapper, just like Jeremy had taught me, then freed my skirt from beneath me. I sat there proud, my back straight. My own horse. I pulled the reins to the right to turn him around and brought my feet in toward the horse, then snapped the reins. He took off at a slow trot, and I rode him to the end of the trail at our farm, pulling the reins taut. I patted his head and turned him back towards Grandpa. I felt like a grown woman, though I would be only twelve in less than a month.

Jeremy walked out of the barn and smiled at me as Emily waved from the porch, a look of awe on her face. I could not wait to show Trapper to Rosa. I could not wait to ride through the meadows with my hair blowing in the wind, like Audrey had all those years before in Indiana.

CHAPTER 29

The spring of 1852 came upon me too soon. The Brandts had packed their wagon, readied the horses and loaded their feed, and given instructions to Abe, who was to be in charge of the farmwork in the Brandts' absence. Rosa told me that her brother, Hans, would travel here every two or three weeks to check on the farm and to pay bills and make needed purchases.

I told Rosa I would visit Abe to make sure he was doing well, and she laughed at me.

"Why are you making fun of me, Rosa?" I asked, puzzled by her reaction.

"Fidelia, you cannot help Abe manage the farmwork. My brother will manage that. You are always mothering, my silly friend."

"Am I? If Abe needs anything, I can tell Grandma. We'll help if we can. Until Hans comes," I said.

Rosa rolled her eyes. My spirited friend was not a helper, but I loved her with her shortcomings, just as she was, just as she loved me.

Missus Brandt, Rosa, and I had gone riding on two occasions just before spring peeked around the corner, before preparations began for their journey. Missus Brandt was quite impressed with how well my new horse rode.

"He is a marvelous horse," said Missus Brandt.

"The best gift I've ever received," I said and stroked

Trapper's neck as we'd galloped along the creek to the east. Nightfall approached in the distance and we turned toward the farmhouse.

"We are all blessed, *mi corazón*," said Missus Brandt.

I straightened my back, modeling Missus Brandt's posture, reflecting her gentle poise and confidence.

"We will miss you, Fidelia, while we are gone. I know that Rosa will miss you dearly."

Again, I felt like family. Ma allowed me to ride to the Brandt farm early, at sunrise, on the day the Brandts departed. Trapper and I followed them, and Bear followed us. I waved as they neared the edge of Austin City, and then I rode home, sad but quite hungry for breakfast. Rosa would be back in late July or August, because her father planned on returning for the harvest. Arriving home, I unsaddled Trapper and led him to his stall, and the smells of bacon and coffee called me into the house.

"Did they leave?" Emily asked.

"Yes, they are on their way," I said. I filled my plate with eggs, bacon, and biscuits, and I joined everyone at the table. It was planting season, so a full day awaited all of us. Ma said we would read in the evening, after supper.

The rains came hard and often in the spring, helping our crops grow thick and high. Grandpa thanked God at supper after each rain. I thought of my friend and her family, wondering how they'd dealt with the storms as they traveled. Wondered if they were safe.

It was an early morning in June, after the crops were in, when Grandpa decided to go fishing.

"Fidelia?" I awoke to the sound of my name being whispered in my ear, but when I opened my eyes it was still dark.

"Fidelia, let's go fishing. At the river," whispered Grandpa, careful not to wake Emily.

I jumped up, pulled on my stockings, threw my old blue cotton dress over my chemise, picked up my shoes, and met Grandpa on the front porch. He already had my horse saddled and our fishing gear, including bait, strapped to his saddle.

"Does Grandma know we're leaving?" I asked.

"Yes, she does. And I've got some biscuits and jam in the saddlebag," he replied as he mounted his horse. When we got to the river, we climbed into Grandpa's old dinghy and off we went. It was a splendid day, not too hot, and after the rains, the fish were plentiful.

"You are becoming a lovely young woman, Fidelia," said Grandpa. "I imagine one day a fancy doctor or lawyer in Austin will snatch you up and take you away."

I looked at Grandpa. *What was he talking about?*

"I'm not going anywhere, Grandpa," I responded. "I'm just a girl."

Grandpa stared at me, but I knew that I had begun to fill out the bodice of my dress, like my friend Rosa. And only three weeks before I'd had my first bleed, and then Mama showed me what to do and how to be discreet. Ma explained the menses to me, but I was certainly in no hurry to become a woman or anyone's wife.

We arrived home after dinner, and Grandpa handed our basket full of fish to Grandma for our supper. Grandma took the basket and looked at me, a frown on her face. Ma sat at the table, and I could see that she'd been crying. I imagined Grandma had caught her taking the medicine again. I walked outside to take my horse to the barn, but Grandpa did not follow me, so I took his horse too.

"Good day, Jeremy," I said as I passed his workshop. "We caught plenty of fish today."

"Great," he said and turned back to his work. I sat on the stool for a moment.

"Uncle Jeremy, I caught the biggest catfish you ever saw."

He turned toward me, and I saw his shiner.

"Not again. What happened to you?" I asked.

"Ah, got in a fight up at the Stagecoach Inn. Some city guy was throwing dice with a bunch of us . . . wanted to quit and walk off with his winnings. With everyone's money."

I sat quiet for a few moments, pondering my sweet uncle's misfortunes.

"Uncle Jeremy, what would we do without you? Everyone 'round here wants the pretty furniture you build. You built me a swing. No—it was three swings."

He said nothing.

"You're a gift to us, Uncle Jeremy."

He was silent for a few minutes.

"From the mouth of a babe," he said, not even looking at me. What an odd day it was, my uncle calling me a baby and Grandpa talking of marrying me off.

He continued his work, so I left him to his sulking. I didn't know where Emily was. I hung up my saddle, brushed Trapper, and brought food to the two horses. I was carrying a bucket of water over to Grandpa's horse when he walked out of the house.

"Fidelia, I need to speak with you. Let's take a walk," he said.

I sat the full bucket near the barn, and we walked toward the big tree where Ma taught our lessons.

"Something has happened," Grandpa said. "Word has come that the Brandt family will not be returning to their home. I've heard they'll be staying in Mexico."

Words escaped me, for I could not believe what I'd heard.

"It is for certain that they are coming back, Grandpa," I said. "Their crops are planted and that is their home, across the fields."

"Family troubles in Mexico have kept them. They must stay, so your friend Rosa will not return." Grandpa said this with such firmness it surprised me.

"Grandpa, I am sure they will return when they can, when things are better again," I said, assuring him.

"Thank you, Fidelia, for putting my horse up. You can sit here and take in the news before helping Grandma in the kitchen." He walked away, then paused and turned. "I'm certain all will be well, Fidelia."

The worried expression on his face did not mirror his words. I wandered toward the pond, thinking maybe Emily was there with Bear. She was not. As I walked back toward the house, I wondered what happened with Missus Brandt's family.

There was little conversation at our evening supper, but the big catfish I had caught was delicious. Grandma had made a pie of wild blackberries and early rhubarb from our garden. My body was filled with weariness from our early day at the river, but I lay awake until almost dawn, worried about Rosa.

As usual, Pa did not accompany us to church on Sunday, but it was good to see my other friends and Pastor Wieland. Normally, there would have been a gleeful sermon as planting season neared an end, but the room, as well as the sermon, was somber.

"We are a saddened community at the loss of our friends, the Brandt family," said the pastor before our last hymn. I looked over at Ma, but she did not return my gaze. I could not understand the sadness, for they would certainly return eventually.

As we visited after church, Betsy Irwin whispered to me. "How awful about your friend Rosa. The whole family."

"What do you mean?" I asked.

"You know. How they died," she said.

"They died?"

"Why, yes. You did not know?" asked Betsy.

I could not breathe. I thought I would faint, but then sucked in air to gain my composure. This could not be true. Grandpa would have told me of such tragedy, but I remembered that Ma had been crying that day I came home from fishing.

Ma called my name as she climbed into our wagon. I climbed in the back with Emily. Tears were gathering in my eyes, but I held my fears inside as we traveled down the trail toward home.

When I walked into the kitchen, I could contain myself no longer.

"Ma, did Rosa die?" I asked.

Ma looked at me. Grandma, putting a pot of water on the stove, looked at Ma.

"What happened?" I screamed, filled with a desperate dread.

"Fidelia, I'm sorry. We did not want to share such tragic news, still not confirmed. We have been told that the Brandt family was killed on their way to the south, south of Fredericksburg," said Ma, her voice trembling.

"Why did Grandpa lie to me?"

"Oh, Fidelia. We did not want to tell you. It is so dreadful, and Rosa was your friend," said Ma.

"Rosa will always be my friend," I yelled, suddenly realizing my face was wet. The tears turned into sobs. I could not stop.

"How did they die?" I asked, after my sobs had eased. "What happened?"

Ma bent to embrace me, held me tight to her chest, when Emily walked into the room.

"What happened?" asked Emily.

Grandma told my sister the news, and then Emily was crying. Grandpa walked in the front door and stood there, his eyes wide open, watching the chaos that filled the room. Still, no one had answered my question.

Grandpa sat at the table, and Grandma put a cup of hot coffee in front of him. His head was bowed.

"Fidelia, I am sorry. I could not make myself tell you such horrible news. But it is now plain that we could not spare you," said Grandpa.

My heart was torn between anger and loss. In spite of Grandpa's lie, I ran to him and hugged him with all my might. I held on tight in search of comfort. I found none.

CHAPTER 30

I cried and tossed all night long. *After the years of losses, my sisters, my aunt, how could this happen? How could God allow this to happen?*

My heart was broken. I will tell you now, as I share my story, that the horrendous loss of my friend, as well as her family, seemed more than a young girl could bear.

My eyes swollen, I sat at the breakfast table with my family as we ate before a day's work. Not a word was spoken. I knew where I was going after breakfast. I helped Grandma with the dishes as Ma went out to weed the garden, then I walked outside and maneuvered through the shrubs and trees toward the Brandt farm. Before I reached the meadow bordering my destination, I heard Emily behind me.

"Fidelia. Wait! Where are you going?" she asked.

I turned to see her running toward me.

"Go home, Em," I yelled back at her. "Tell Ma I'll be back shortly to finish my chores."

A pout replaced Emily's habitual smile, and she stood and watched me walk away. I saw the cotton fields across the meadow, the cotton plants thick and green, and then I saw Abe walking toward the barn. As I neared, I saw a man standing on the porch at the house. It appeared he was reading something and did not see me.

I met up with Abe at the back of the barn.

"G'day, Fidelia. I'm surprised to see you. You well?" asked Abe.

Before I could say anything, I felt tears, unable to hold them back. I stuttered, trying to release my words.

"Abe. Abe . . . what happened to Rosa?" I asked.

"Oh, dear, girl. I don't wanna even talk about it."

I stared at him, unable to speak.

"Oh, sweet girl. The pain in your eyes is hurtin' me. It was terrible. I heard the news from young Master Hans. He said the Injuns attacked the family after they passed through Fredricksburg, killing Master Brandt first. Master Hans told me they shot his mother as she ran through the trees, and Rosa was missing. The master said it looked like they, the Injuns, took her."

"Rosa is still alive?"

"No, ma'am. She ain't."

I stared again. Just stared, as chills ran down my back. Abe looked down at the ground. He clearly did not want to tell me more.

"Rosa. Sweet Rosa. Master Hans told me jus' this morning that a settler from Medina found Rosa's body by Seco Creek. Word came early today, before dawn."

I gasped before the sobs bellowed from me. I fell down on my knees. I felt Abe touch my head.

"Dear, Fidelia. God has her now. I's so sorry. So sorry."

"What's all the commotion here?" I looked up to see the man I'd seen on the porch, clearly Rosa's brother, though he looked nothing like my friend but more like her father.

My eyes were distorted by tears, but I could see that Hans was a tall man. As my eyes focused, I saw that he had flaxen-colored hair, pale blue eyes, and was thin, yet he appeared to be a strong man, like his father.

"Who is this, Abe?" he asked.

"I am Fidela," I said. "Rosa's friend, from the farm over there." I pointed through the trees.

"Ah. Mama has written me of you, in her letters," he said, his eyes softened. "I am Hans, Rosa's brother."

"Sorry, Master," said Abe in a pitch weaker than his usual voice. "I told her what happened. She begged to know."

"You should have sent her to the house, Abe," said Hans, his eyes narrowing. "Come, Fidelia. Reka is in the kitchen, and I will tell her to prepare you a cup of citrus or water. Come."

He turned toward the house, and I followed. Before I entered the house, I looked over my shoulder to see Abe standing where we'd left him, watching us. In the dining room, I sat at the familiar table, and when Hans returned to the table with a cup, he sat down across from me.

"I've come to oversee the farm for now," he said. "We buried my ma and pa in Austin. Sadly, Rosa's already buried in Bandera, I'm told."

My tears started again, and Hans handed me a handkerchief. Once I'd dried my eyes, I could see that Hans's eyes were reddened, and I realized that he, too, had been crying.

"Will you stay here . . . at the farm?" I asked.

"No. I have a farm to the northeast. I do not believe I can manage both, but I will have to decide what to do."

I was afraid to ask any more questions, for I was fearful to hear the answers, but my curiosity was greater than my fear.

"Did the Indians hurt Rosa? Did they kill her?" I asked.

"Child, I don't know. Just got the news of her being

found and buried. The Bandera sheriff sent word to me after he heard of the attack near Fredericksburg and the missing girl. Said he'd tell me more after he speaks with the man who found her."

I wanted to talk to Rosa, but I could never do that again. I felt alone in a big world. I looked at Hans and saw that he was a handsome man. I handed him my cup and thanked him for his kindness.

"I need to get home and help my ma. Got chores," I said, and turned to leave.

"I am pleased to meet you, Fidelia. Having now met you makes me realize that my sister was growing up into a young woman, and that I've been neglectful in not visiting more often. Our family is blessed that she had such a dear friend."

I looked at him and stared for a moment, for I could find no words to say. I was but an empty shell.

I walked out the door, but I was not going home. I walked past the barn and the slave cabins, on to the old cemetery in the weeds. There, with other grown-over graves, was Abby's stone:

Abigail
Died 1850
99 yrs

Abe regularly weeded her grave and set in cuttings from Missus Brandt's rosebush. There were small pink buds, and I imagined one day this would be a magnificent rosebush. *But would Abe be here to see it? To care for it?* I had not asked Hans that question.

I sat in front of Abby's grave marker. I needed to talk to

Abby, but everyone one was gone. My aunt, my friend, Abby. My family had lied to me. God had failed me, if there even was a god.

"Oh, Abby. Were you here, you would comfort me, tell me why. I know you would," I said, speaking to a tombstone, to my old friend who could no longer answer me. "Everyone leaves. They die and go to heaven, or so I'm told, so why shouldn't I go to heaven?"

"You're too young to go to heaven," whispered a voice behind me. I jumped and turned to find Abe standing there.

"Rosa was young. So young, like me," I said.

"Yes, she was, but she didn't choose to go to heaven. The Comanche took it away from her, her decision. I hear 'twas Comanche renegades. Don't know for sure. You can't choose to leave, 'cause you still are a light in this world."

I stared at Abe. He sounded like Abby.

"You know Abby woulda wanted you to grow up, have babies, fall in love, and someday be as old as she was."

"But everyone I love dies, Abe."

"Everyone Abby loved, 'cept me, died. But she lit the world for most of a hundred years. Don't know what I'd a done without her. One day you'll have a grandson who feels that way 'bout you."

Again, I stared at Abe. Nothing sounded true anymore. Words just rattled around, bouncing off lies and platitudes. Off of promises. I didn't know who to believe. Abe reached down his hand to help me up.

"Is Hans going to sell you, Abe? Or is he gonna free you?" I asked.

Now it was his turn to stare. His eyes looked to the side, for he had no answer for me.

"Good day, Abe. I'm going home," I said, and walked

away.

I arrived home in time to help Grandma prepare dinner. I felt different inside. Just different, but I could not say how. I spoke to no one the rest of the day, except Emily. After supper, Ma sat down at the table with paper and began writing a letter to her sister back in Indiana.

"Ma, what are you writing about to Aunt Anna?" I asked.

"I am going to tell her how you girls are growing up too fast, how the black mare foaled last week. I'll tell her what crops are growing this year."

"Aren't you going to tell her about Rosa? The Brandts?" I asked.

"Mercy, Fidelia. I may mention it, but we don't know much about the details of what happened on the trail. About who did it. I will tell her of our sorrowful loss," said Ma. "I hear you met Hans Brandt over at the farm."

I wondered how she knew that. He must have stopped by when I was doing chores, or maybe Grandpa went over to visit him.

"Yes, Ma. I did. I wonder what he will do with the farm. What he'll do with the three slaves."

"I don't know, Fidelia. Time will reveal that, I'm certain," she said, and returned to her task, taking pen to paper. "I will tell your cousin Jane that you send your regards. Jeremy said he would post the letter for me tomorrow in Brushy."

In our room that evening, as we readied for bed, Emily asked where I'd gone in the morning. Her voice trembled when she spoke to me.

"I had to find out what happened. To Rosa. Everyone's

keeping secrets," I answered.

"What did happen, Fidelia?"

"Rosa is dead. It was the Indians, and I don't want to talk about it."

I washed my face in the basin and hung my dress on a peg. Emily's mouth turned downward, her eyes watered. I did not know if it was the news that saddened her or if she was upset that I wouldn't talk to her. I did not care.

CHAPTER 31

I fell asleep, though I had not planned to, and I woke in the middle of the night. There was a crescent moon in the sky, giving me just enough light for travel. I dressed, taking extra stockings and a dress, and I put my shawl and a cotton blanket into my satchel. I picked up my boots, then tiptoed to the kitchen. I put a cup in my satchel and grabbed some jerky from where Grandma stashed it. As I walked toward the back door, I turned around to the kitchen and picked up one of Grandma's paring knives, not her favorite one, and slipped it into my satchel.

I wasn't taking my horse, for I did not want to be tracked, and I closed Bear in an empty horse stall, for I knew he would follow me and reveal my whereabouts. I could walk to the creek in the dark, but I knew I needed a lantern, something Rosa and I always coveted when we were at the cave. I took the lantern in the workshop, and when I saw Jeremy's flint lying next to it, I put that in the pocket of my dress. I filled the lantern with oil so that it would last long. Once done, I sat down and put on my boots, then headed through the trees toward the meadows, where I would walk on toward Brushy Creek and our cave.

At the edge of the meadow, I stopped to light the lantern. I'd heard noises of the night and wanted to see my way and warn critters of my approach. I walked unhurriedly, for I didn't want to tire myself. It was a lengthy distance to the creek, especially on foot. I could think of nothing except Rosa and how alone I was. I thought of Emily and how I'd turned my back on her last night. Grandpa would be worried, as would Ma and Grandma, but, strangely, none of that mattered to me.

When I came to the cedar brake, I walked around its edge, avoiding the dense brush. Then I came upon the creek's edge suddenly and walked westward toward the cave opening. The creek's water was low, and the lantern eased my way into the cave. I was numb. I didn't know my own self, but I knew I was fatigued beyond my thoughts. I brushed small stones to the side and spread my shawl on the cave's floor near the moss, rolled my cloak into a pillow, and extinguished the flame in the lantern. In spite of my misery, sleep found me quickly. When I woke, morning light had crept into the cave from above and two chickadees were chirping melodically to one another. The earth seemed good for only a moment, until I remembered all that had driven me here to this sanctuary. Rosa's and my secret place.

I sat up, seeing my dress was rumpled and my hair snarled. I had forgotten a hairbrush. As I sat, waking my senses and feeling a thirst, I expected to hear voices calling my name. But there were no voices. Only the birdsong and the hint of running water, so I rose and changed into the frock I'd thrown into my satchel. I grabbed my cup and my soiled dress, not bothering to light the lantern, and I felt my way out of the dark cave.

I realized I was hungry but had left the jerky in my bag. I scooped water from the running creek into my cup, gulping it down as I looked around me to see only the familiar stillness of the creek. I dipped my soiled dress into the creek and rubbed it, leaving it draped on a tree limb as I splashed water on my face. I could not let it lay in the sun. It would be a sign of my presence here, so after I refilled my cup, I carried the wet dress back into the cave with me and spread it over a large rock to dry.

I pulled the jerky from my bag and sat there in the dim light, pulling bites from the dried pork. My thoughts began to churn again. My first thoughts went to my family, who were most certainly frantic about my absence. Or maybe they had not noticed my absence, but only thought I was about my chores. Guilt filled me until I remembered they had lied to me, until I remembered what happened to Rosa.

I tried to sort my feelings, but I had lost myself. Nothing made sense, and moments came and went when I just wanted to lay in the dark and die. I was different, but not in a good way. I wanted a path, needed direction, but instead, I slept.

I woke as the sun was falling to the west, behind the large willow above, and the cave was dark. Suddenly, I thought of poor Missus and Mister Brandt when I remembered that the boys at church had spoken of how some Comanche took the scalps of those they'd slain. I sat up in the darkness and gasped at my mind's image of beautiful Missus Brandt without her long black hair, then I shook the frightful vision from my head. I felt for the flint and struck it to light the lantern.

I pulled the rest of the jerky out of the bag and finished it greedily, as if there were a need to share. Rosa came to mind, not only thoughts of her, but her image as well, as if she were sitting with me. She sat, cross-legged, looking at me. Her black hair was pulled into two buns, her cheeks as rosy as life itself, framing a mischievous smile, as was her custom.

I spoke as if we were hiding together in our cave, as if she were truly with me.

"Oh, Rosa. You are so beautiful and happy. How could you leave me when you had promised to return? How?"

I sat and watched her as if she could answer. But she could not. She was only a vision.

"I've lost so much, Rosa," I uttered in a soft voice. "My baby sisters, my Aunt Audrey, my innocence, and my faith. Now you."

I reached out to touch my friend's hand but pulled back, afraid of the truth.

"With each goodbye, I've questioned God and received no answer. Now I hate him."

I shuddered. I had said it out loud, about God. As I sat in the cool dampness, I looked up and wondered if the cave would crumble, then realized that I was alone. My mind went to ghosts for, though I'd never had beliefs of their presence, I remembered feeling such a presence in the forests of the Ozarks. *Was Rosa a ghost? Had Rosa really visited me?* I remembered the arrowhead I'd found near the Ozark trail and then remembered I'd put it in my satchel all those years ago.

I rummaged through the bag and there, in a pocket, was the old stone. I pulled it out and, as it lay in my palm, ran my finger over it. I wished it to be magic, to return Rosa and her family. In the dimness of the cave it did not even sparkle and was as silent as God. I held it near the lantern and turned it over to reveal the glassy quartz reflecting the light, as if it held life in some form.

I liked being alone here. It was comforting, unlike the quiet between Ma and Pa. Unlike all the lies and false comfort. Different from the noise of constant farmwork.

Night was coming, and I was not sleepy. Holding the lantern, I found my way to the cave's exit and, leaving the lantern there, climbed out and sat on the large tree roots. I listened to the creek's water, what little there was, gurgle over the smoothed stones of the creek bed.

I tried not to think of my family. I am certain they were worried, fretting about where I went. Searching. I'd heard no one call my name. I had no idea where I was headed, what I was searching for in this cave alone, for a palsy yet held me in its grip.

With a suddenness, Rosa's scent filled my nostrils and her voice called to me as I sat by the creek, this place that had nearly killed both of us the last time we were here. *Would that have been a mercy?*

I heard the call of coyotes in the distance. I wanted to be part of them, a pack. I wanted to be the dripping water cooling my feet, part of the sliver of moon grasped in the tree branches. I wanted to be here, right here, forever.

Normally, the wail of a coyote would send me for cover, but not tonight. Tonight, I felt free of fear, for it was probable that my best friend had lived and died through the worst that could happen. One thing I knew for certain: death was inescapable. I was no longer a child believing in fairy tales.

I sat breathing in the night breeze, my feet tickled by the light drip of water over the stones. I sat there for hours until the call of an owl in the tree above me brought me to my feet. I looked up, attempting to find him, but saw nothing and heard the faintest rustle of leaves.

I returned to the cave. It must have been the wee hours of the night, but I did not know. Time seemed endless here.

I rearranged the blanket and extinguished the lantern. Thoughts of Aunt Audrey passed through my mind as I lay my head on my folded cloak, remembrances of her excursion into the woods. And just before sleep took me, I remembered I had no more food.

Chapter 32

I awoke with a start at hearing a noise from the creek. I sat up, listened. It was the gait of a horse splashing through water, following the creek away from our farm. I heard no one call, and I knew the rider was alone. The sound of the hooves moved away from me, from the cave. Because of the early hour, I suspected it was Jeremy or Pa. A part of me wanted to run to greet him, another part was fearful it might be a stranger, and the part of me that brought me to the cave only wanted to stay hidden. So I did.

I could see a faintness of dawn by the light streaming in. The sounds moved farther and farther away. I stripped down to my chemise and crept to the exit, holding my soiled clothes, my stockings. I felt tired.

Listening carefully to ensure I was alone, I placed my soiled clothes in the water, rubbing them against the stones, and then laid them on a large rock at the creek side. On the other side of the rock, at the base of the large cypress, I found the water was deep enough for me to sit in it. I dunked my head beneath the water to clean my hair, and perhaps to cleanse my soul. In places it was deeper than I thought. Opening my eyes, I saw fish swimming about. They surprised me, for the water flowing in the creek was so shallow, but there was a pool at the edge where rock rimmed the creek, its depth dug by erosion over time. I was hungry and resolute.

I submerged under the water again and tried to grab a perch. It was small and slipped right out of my hands, and I skinned my knee on the rough creek bottom. I tried three more times before I succeeded in grasping the prize and tossing it away from the creek.

I shook the water from me like a dog would and climbed back down into the cave. I gathered from my bag the knife, the flint, my cup, and my extra stockings, and I wrapped it all in my shawl.

Back by the creek, I tied the shawl over my still-damp chemise. I gathered some small dead branches and kindling from around the trees and bushes, stacking them, as Grandpa had taught me, like a tall triangle on bare soil near the creek.

The hapless perch no longer flopped about in search of its survival, and I took the knife and cut off the head and fins, then scraped the scales from the fish before slicing it down the center, pulling out the innards and spine. Finding a thin branch, I broke the end and pierced the fish before starting a fire with the flint. That would be my breakfast.

Pulling pieces of the tender fish from the stick, I satiated my hunger as I listened to the sounds around me. I heard nothing but the birdsong and squirrels running through the trees. I wondered if Pa would be proud of my wilderness skills, but I knew he was likely cursing my name instead.

Once satiated, I put out the fire, splashed some water about the ashes, and covered any traces of my meal. I'd laid out my washed clothes to dry and sat in a sunny spot until my chemise and hair were dry. I could tell it would be a sunny day, for the winter sky was a cloudless blue.

I wondered if I should move on. I did not relish the idea of running away from home, encountering strangers who might mean harm. What I wanted most was peace, but I had not yet found a salve for my misery, as I thought I would. What I wanted was for Rosa to be here with me. Not her ghost, but my friend in flesh.

Once I was dry, I ran my fingers through my hair, and decided to go without my stockings, which would only get soiled and snagged. I carried my belongings down into the cave, and when I climbed up again to gather my washed clothes, I vomited into the creek. And again, once more. The suddenness of it frightened me, and I splashed water onto my face and into my mouth to freshen myself. After catching and cleaning perch, gratifying my hunger, my stomach was again empty. I gathered the damp clothes I'd laid on the rock and my clean dress, taking them below.

I did not feel well, and I wondered if the fish had not set well with me. I wished I'd had my aunt's book of poetry to read, but the light was really too dim, and nausea consumed me, so I lay down and wrapped myself in my shawl. I began to shiver. I woke in the late afternoon, and though my stomach rumbled, I was not hungry but hot and thirsty.

I quenched my thirst at the creek and it took all my strength to return to the cave. I worried as time passed toward night, worried that I should be home if I'm ill. I was not willing to admit I might need my mother, but I was too weary to return home and still too filled with sadness to want to. I slept.

By morning I was sleeping and tossing back and forth. I was certain I had a fever and could tell the sky above was clouded. I knew I needed my ma and decided I would leave soon. I fell into a feverish sleep.

I never heard the approaching horse as rain began to fall. I never felt the dampness in the cave as water dripped on the stone walls. I felt the touch of a hand.

"Fidelia. Wake up."

It was Pa's voice. His hand covered my forehead. It felt cool.

"You are ill, girl. We have looked everywhere for you," he said, and I heard the distress in his voice. I heard his words shake, as if distant, and felt his arms lift me. Raindrops cooled my face as Pa raised me, too weak to even hold my head upright. He sat me upon his horse, holding me seated in front of him as he guided the horse toward home.

I awoke in darkness in my own bed, alone in my room, but heard Ma and Grandma busying themselves beyond the door. *Where was Emily?* Her bed was empty. The door opened, and Ma came carrying a basin of water.

"You are awake," she said.

"Where's Em?" I asked.

"She is sleeping in my room. I don't want her to catch what is making you sick. Let's get you well before we ask you why you ran off like that," said Ma.

"Pa brought me home."

"Yes, dear. He did. He was filled with fear of what might have happened to you. He'd even accused Hans Brandt of taking you. But you are home now. And you need rest."

I wanted to tell Ma everything, the depth of my sorrow, but weakness consumed me and sleep beckoned.

Grandma walked in with a cup of hot tea, not a

common drink in our home, but it warmed my throat. Ma caressed my face and neck with cool rags. I dozed toward a fitful sleep where I dreamt, where I envisioned the trees over the cave, whispering to each other in the roots near me. *Did trees speak to each other? As if conniving my well-being, as if sending signals?* In my dream, they did not seem evil, but nurturing. Nevertheless, the dreams gave no comfort.

My fever broke in the morning, and Ma brought me breakfast in bed. Emily visited.

"Ma? How did Pa find me?" I asked.

"Well, I don't understand why you left, daughter. We were all so distraught. But your pa, beside himself, found help at the Brandt farm, from Abe."

"From Abe?"

"Yes. Nothing had helped to find you, not even sending your dog out to search. But Abe suggested that Pa take Pedro, the horse you would ride at the Brandt farm. He said that you girls would ride off through the woods and be gone for hours. Pa told us that he eased the reins and let the horse go as he wished, as Abe had advised him, and your pa ended up at the creek, near that cave where Pa found you."

"Oh, Mama. I'm sorry. Sorry I worried you."

"You could have died there, Fidelia!" Ma's eyes watered.

"I know," I whispered. "I was lost, Ma. I still am. I feel empty inside. Without Rosa, I feel older and sadder . . . and lost."

CHAPTER 33

Jeremy had gone to the cave and brought back all my things, all that he could find. The clothes were muddied, as was my satchel, because rainwater had covered the floor of the cave after Pa had found me. Jeremy never found his flint that I'd taken, but the rest came home and was laundered. I was glad that I had slipped the arrowhead back into my bag.

Two days after my fever broke, I was up early to milk the cows when Grandpa walked into the barn.

"Get the bait basket and your fishing pole. We are going fishing after breakfast," he said to me.

It was a hot June day, and Grandpa maneuvered the dinghy at the river toward the thick trees blocking morning's sun. We baited our lines and waited in the quiet. It wasn't long before I got a bite. The early shade called the bass to their fates and filled our basket.

We sat in silence as I watched the gauzy damselflies flit over the surface of the river's water. Grandpa cut some heavy string and tied the basket over the side of the boat.

"I want to talk to you, Fidelia, about what happened," he said.

"About what, Grandpa?" I asked, knowing well what he spoke about, but defying any talk of it. Grandpa sat quiet for a moment.

"What made you run away, hide in that cave, child?"

Now, I paused again.

"Fidelia, I know the depth of your pain in losing your friend. We both know how much loss our family has endured. But why did you feel the need to leave your home? Your family?" asked Grandpa, his voice so soft, as if we were still luring the fish to us.

I did not know how to answer. I wanted to forget. Everything. Minutes passed. Grandpa said nothing, still awaiting my answer.

"I don't know, Grandpa," I said, hoping the matter would fade to another topic, like how Grandma might cook the fish for supper. What the weather would be tomorrow. But I knew he would not let it go.

"You know. Dig deeper, child."

"I could not bear what happened to my friend, Grandpa, what happened to her family. I felt empty inside. I still feel empty." I looked at Grandpa, meeting his sad eyes.

"The cave was our secret place, Grandpa," I whispered. "I felt near Rosa there. I wanted to be near her, even in death."

Death. As soon as that word escaped my mouth, my tears began to fall.

Grandpa reached for my hand, squeezed it.

"Dear Delia," he said, using the name Grandma used. "None of us could bear your death, another loss . . . any more than you can bear Rosa's death. Your pa was beside himself, and if he had not gone to Hans and Abe, we might have lost you as well."

I thought of the evening Pa found me, how feeble I was. The water seeping into the cave. I was surprised that it was Pa who found me.

"I know you think your pa doesn't care about you girls, but he does," said Grandpa, as if he'd read my mind. "His struggle being here in Texas is not lost on me. He not only loves you, Fidelia, but he is afraid of losing another daughter."

He paused a moment.

"I imagine that he, too, feels empty after losing two daughters and his sister."

"But, Grandpa, everyone lied to me about Rosa. About God and about heaven. No gracious God would take away the ones we love. Where is He, this God you and Grandma talk about?"

"Dear, I have questioned my faith, just as you do," said Grandpa, without hesitation, as if he'd foreseen my doubt. "But over time, I've come to know that God is everywhere. He is in this drop of water," he said as he dipped his hand over the side of the boat and let the water drip from his fingers. "In our hearts, in our ancestors who have carried us here and are buried in the earth. He is the belief we have in tomorrow and in forever."

I looked at Grandpa as I tried to understand his words, but they fell hollow to my ears.

"But why did he take Rosa? And Maureen? Aunt Audrey? All of them? Hester?" I asked.

"No one is promised a new day, child. That is why God wants us to live each day as if it were our whole life. For it's a gift. And Rosa was a gift. Soon it will be time to embrace a new friend and be a gift to them, as Rosa was for you."

I dipped my hand in the cool river water, running it along as it broke the reflection of the clouds in the sky. It was all connected, and I watched the clouds waver in the water.

Grandpa pulled the basket into the boat and pulled up his anchor. We headed for the shore and our horses, where we gave them some water from Grandpa's wooden bucket.

We rode a while in silence.

"I know you feel different, Fidelia. But I pray you never turn away from your family again, but, instead reach out to us for comfort. You'll be a young woman soon enough, if this recent calamity has not made you so."

It was only two days later when, at dinner, Grandpa said Hans Brandt was selling the farm.

"What will he do with the slaves?" I asked.

"He said he planned on selling them, hopefully to the new owner," said Grandpa.

I looked at Grandpa in disgust. This cannot happen, I thought, but I knew better than to speak of this during our meal.

"Can we not add the property to ours?" asked Grandma.

"I've pondered such, but we can hardly manage what we have. Since I've purchased this farm from old man Brown, buying another farm would be a large investment. Likely more debt. And then there would be the extra work and cost of farming that land." Grandpa looked at my pa. "Maybe you could buy it, John? But the state would give you so much more land if you can get a grant."

"I'm not wanting the Brandt farm. I still want a grant of land near the river, Father. If I'm staying in Texas," said Pa, who then looked over at Ma. I did not embrace the sound of those last words I heard. I'd never thought of Pa leaving. *Or did he mean the family, without my grandparents?*

After we finished our meal, I followed Grandpa to the barn.

"Grandpa, you told me to come to you if I needed help or comfort," I said as he stopped by the hay bales, giving me his full attention. "They cannot sell the Brandt slaves. Missus Brandt wanted them set free."

"Fidelia, I don't think Hans is of a mind to set them free. If nothing else, he'd take them to his plantation, but he told me he needs no more mouths to feed. Doesn't need 'em, he said."

Grandpa looked at me and saw the set of my jaw, the fervor in my eyes.

"I could buy them . . . or negotiate a deal. But I'll not have slaves. I'd have to pay them. Maybe house them. Not sure I need the help. There's three of them, right? What with Abe's new wife."

"Yes, Grandpa," I replied.

I could see in Grandpa's eyes that thoughts were churning in his head.

"Fidelia, I'll talk to Hans. I don't think he'll free 'em. He's firmly immersed in his profits, but I will speak to him."

"Thank you, Grandpa," I said, and hugged him until he told me I had to let go.

Christmas came with freezing temperatures, but with no snow like we'd always welcomed for Christmas up north. This year we had a tree filled with ornaments in our sitting room. Pa had finally relented. After our gifts had been shared on Christmas morning, Grandpa asked Emily to go to the barn with him. I had seen a new horse, a handsome gray dun in the barn, so I followed them, suspecting Emily was about to get her own horse. Wasn't I surprised when Grandpa took her to a corner, behind hay bales, where the mewling welcomed us before we saw the black and white kittens. Three of them. Bear, who followed me, wagged his tail and inched forward to see the critters. He sniffed each one and walked away.

"Emily, these are your cats to care for," Grandpa said. "To feed and keep track of. They will be barn cats, but they are yours, so take good care of them. You have to be sure you lock them up in the barn at night, or the owls or coyotes will get them. You can name them as you like. The Harris family, from the inn, had more kittens than they could keep. Merry Christmas, granddaughter."

Emily hardly heard Grandpa's words, for she was picking up each kitten, petting it, then catching the one getting away.

"Can they come in the house, Grandpa?" Emily asked.

"No, Emily. They are barn cats. If we let them in the house, Grandma will be chasing me with that big iron skillet of hers."

Then Emily was giggling. I joined in, visualizing such a scene in the yard.

"Fidelia, I have something for you," said Grandpa as I followed him back to the house, leaving Emily with her new kittens.

Grandpa walked to the corner of the sitting room, by a window, where there sat a small table recently finished by

Uncle Jeremy. I recalled seeing it unfinished in the workshop.

"This is yours. Your desk. And I had Jeremy find this leather-bound journal for you at the print shop in Austin. Here is a steel pen and a vessel of ink."

"To write what, Grandpa?" I asked.

"To write down your thoughts, your feelings. To write poems and your memories of Rosa and Audrey and all that matters to you. Fill it with your words, Fidelia." Grandpa winked.

I picked up the pen, ran my fingers over it, then turned the pages of the journal, each one blank. I had never thought of writing my own poems.

"Fidelia, I know the new school is built, and you girls will start classes next month. They are gathering a small library, where you can borrow books to read. You will have poetry books to read, like your Aunt Audrey had."

"I will write it all down, Grandpa. I will." I don't know why I said those words, for I was skeptical. *What would I write? Would my written words matter?* Yet I thanked Grandpa and hugged him, for I was filled with gratitude for his reassurance, for his faith in me.

The next day, in the afternoon as the sun shone in the window and onto my new desk, I sat and dipped the nib of the steel pen into the ink. It felt powerful, but then I realized that I would need something to wipe the steel nib. I found some fabric scraps to use, and then began writing, suddenly grateful for Ma making me practice my penmanship on the slates. I started penning my memories of Indiana, the distant and brief memories of my baby sister Hester, our fields of beans and corn that crossed to Uncle Levi's farm. I wrote of playing hide and seek with my cousin Jane amidst the tall corn. Jane, who I remembered only as a little girl but who had certainly grown as I had. I knew I could fill a book of our wagon journey through Missouri and Arkansas. And the words spilled.

By the end of the week, I knew that I would likely need more journals. There was so much to tell, so many stories. I had never felt so full, so confident. All these years later, I can see that my feelings, all of my words, written were of worth as I now unfold my family's story. Our story through the eyes of a naïve and determined girl.

CHAPTER 34

At the end of January, the days still cold, Emily and I were filled with excitement as Ma packed us each a lunch. Our new school was nearby, but Emily and I rode together on my horse. I tethered Trapper to the rail in front of the school as some other children had done, and we walked in to find our seats.

There were no girls in class older than me, now thirteen. I realized how fortunate I was that Pa had allowed me to attend school, for he deeply believed education was wasted on girls, but Ma had prevailed, likely with some help from Grandma. I sat to the side of the class, not wanting to draw attention to myself. There was one boy my age and an older boy, Nathaniel, in class. They sat in the back row, and I was certain they'd be gone when planting started in the spring.

Emily and I knew several children from our church, and the room was filled with a buzz of excitement. Though the older boys would disappear soon enough, we were all together and eager to learn. Along the wall I saw two bookcases with the books Grandpa had told me would be there. I was seated right next to them and read the titles. Poets Cliffton and Wordsworth stared back at me from the shelf. And Lord Byron, the very collection I'd placed in my aunt's coffin, sat on the shelf within my reach. Books authored by Poe and Dickens and Anderson, and more, sat next to the poetry. I had never before read a novel or a story, except from the Bible.

Our new teacher, Miss Lerner, introduced herself to us. She wore eyeglasses, which made her look smart, and she was so tiny that Henry, only ten, stood taller than her. She was dressed smartly in a dark blue flannel dress tied at the neckline with a black satin bow and drawn in at the waist, emphasizing her fine figure. Her dark hair was pulled back with a ribbon and then fell free, and she had the bluest eyes, made bigger by the glasses she wore. There were about sixteen students, and I wondered if she'd be able to keep the class focused, especially the young ones. I'd heard of teachers having switches, but I did not see one.

She soon proved her tiny frame held a mighty spirit. Schooling was her focus, and if any of us interfered with it, a reprimand was swift and firm. Miss Lerner was to become a special guidance in my life as time revealed to her that my interest in writing and reading was akin to her own. She suggested books from the shelves for me to take home and read, and I must admit, I enjoyed those stories and poetry collections more than the Bible verses in my bedside book.

My sweet sister had little curiosity in the books I brought home, in the poems I attempted to pen. With her affable personality, friends came to her easily at school. She was eager to help Miss Lerner with social events, with organizing games at play. I didn't think I'd ever have a friend like Rosa again and envied my sister's ease with people. Yet I was blessed to have Emily. She lit our house with her giggles and her happiness, and God knew how much our family needed that light.

Since coming to Texas, there had been a couple of years when Pa and Grandpa had eked out little profit, but Grandpa's frugal ways had kept us fed and clothed through each year. Then came the years when profits allowed us some frivolities or a new buggy, new tools for Jeremy, or ink and stationery for me. The last season had been one of those years, but in spite of that, Grandma always pinched pennies and kept our root cellar filled and ready for the years that would prove difficult.

Grandpa told me that Hans Brandt was staying at the neighboring farm for a while and that he'd not yet found a buyer. He shared with me that he'd had conversations with the young man about the slaves, but Hans was adamant that they would stay with the farm.

"But, Grandpa," I moaned.

"Don't you worry yet. We're still talking to each other." He winked at me. "I can be just as persistent as you."

Through the spring, I was diligent in doing my homework. Emily did the bare minimum, but her charm coupled with turning in middling papers allowed her to pass. By the end of the school session, there were only four young boys and the seven girls, with the exception of twelve-year-old Susanna, who left to help her ma with a new baby.

On the Sunday before school dismissed, our church held its annual picnic at Brushy Creek. As Emily and her girlfriends played a game amidst the trees, I sat alone by the creek, having removed my shoes and stockings to dip my feet in the coolness of the water as it flowed downstream toward the cave. The creek always brought thoughts of Rosa and our adventures.

Pastor Wieland sat down beside me, resting his feet on

a tree root.

"Good day, Fidelia," he said.

"Good afternoon, Pastor Wieland."

"It is cool here, near the water," he said, and he held his hand in the stream as the water flowed and wrapped about his fingers.

"Are you doing well? I know you have missed your friend," he said.

Surprised by his directness, I turned and looked at him.

"I know what happened last summer, after we lost the Brandt family," he said. "I helped your grandpa and pa search for you and was beyond relief when you were found. I know you suffered greatly, Fidelia. You have looked happier these last couple of months, but I fear you may be hiding lingering heartache. Am I right?"

I dug my toes into the pebbles beneath the water.

"I am managing well, Pastor," I said, but he remained quiet. I watched the water move, and the silence begged me to speak.

"Yes, sir, I am still sad. As if there is a dead part in my heart that still sits there, confused. But I am strong." As those words left my mouth, I remembered Gray Feather and his words to me so long ago. "Grandpa has encouraged me to write my thoughts, and I find it gives me comfort. A path to understanding."

"That is wise. I know you're strong, Fidelia, but God does not want you to be alone," said Pastor Wieland.

"But He took her. And her family," I said, without hesitation, challenging him as I turned to face him. "He takes everyone."

A strong breeze rustled the leaves, and I felt an eeriness. The pastor paused long before speaking.

"He does take everyone, Fidelia. For we are His. But He loves you as He loved Rosa, and I am certain He expects much of you, for you have shown Him how capable you are. Like how you stand firm for Abe's freedom. How you help your family at the farm. How you gave so much comfort to old Abby at the Brandt farm. You are a gift, dear girl. A gift to all of us."

He rose to his feet. I wondered how he knew about Abe. And Abby.

"Don't forget it," he said with a slow and firm voice, and walked away. My posture straightened. I looked to the sky and watched the small finches dart from tree to tree. Sat with the gurgling water for a time before I joined my family in the meadow.

On the last day of school, we wished Miss Lerner a good summer, and I begged her to return in the fall. She promised that she would, and Emily and I returned home knowing we'd be given more chores through summer. In my hand I carried the book Miss Lerner allowed me to keep until school started again, Elizabeth Barrett Browning's *Sonnets from the Portuguese*. Love poems would consume my summer.

CHAPTER 35

"Em," I said. "Hey, Em. Do you think Papa wishes I'd been a boy?"

"That's silly, Fidelia. Never."

"Well, he's always saying he needed sons to help in the fields."

"You help. We both have our chores," said Emily.

"All Mama ever had were girls. But the babies are sleeping in the graveyard. I remember so little about our sister Hester that Ma buried back in Indiana and you probably don't remember little Maureen. She was just a baby when she got the fever, right after we got to Texas. Just girls . . . now, just you and me. No boys for Pa," I said as I gathered my skirt and climbed one branch higher in the looming oak tree with its branches twisted perfect and broad for climbing.

"I remember Maureen," said Emily, challenging my remark. She was now eleven and set in her ways and opinions. "Fidelia, you'd better get down from up there. You're way too old to be up in that tree, and you'll tear your dress."

It was a warm June day, and we had sat under the big tree that morning reading the Bible with Ma. She'd left us in the meadow when she walked to the house to make dinner. The clang of the dinner bell would likely sound any minute now, and from up in the tree, I could see the dust stirred by Pa's horse coming down the road. He had gone into Austin City again to search for a grant of land near Cypress Creek. As he neared, the frown on his face conveyed he'd been unsuccessful in his search, but he was here just in time for our midday meal.

"Pa, when will we move into our own home? By the big creek?" asked Emily, breaking some bread for the jam.

"Oh, dear, it will be a while. You and Fidelia might be young women before we find our land. Right, John?" said Ma.

"Nothin' wrong with you living here," growled Pa.

Emily and I looked at each other as I pulled a face.

"Fidelia said you wished she were a boy, Pa," said Emily.

I glared at Emily, and Pa glared at us and asked Ma for some more ale. Ma gave us a look, a glance that said *behave yourselves*, and we finished our meal in silence. After dinner, Emily and I took the dirty dishes to the tin basin in the kitchen and ran to our bedroom, where I pulled the poetry book from the shelf and read love poems to her as she rolled her eyes and chortled.

With the work Jeremy had been doing for the Harris family up at the Stagecoach Inn, he'd become smitten with Matilda. She was the daughter of a regular stage driver and had been given room and board in return for her help in the kitchen, mostly because Mister Harris had only sons, no daughters. When I'd hang out in the workshop with Jeremy, he was constantly talking about Matilda.

"Fidelia, she cooks most of day for the boarders at the

inn. Sometimes her hair is loose and falls in waves almost to her waist, beautiful auburn waves."

"You must be in love," I said, teasing him. Though he really did sound like he was in love.

"Don't be silly, Fidelia. I'm in no hurry to get wed," he replied.

"Well, you're old enough," I said, then laughed.

"How can I tell if she likes me?"

"Uncle Jeremy, I can't tell you. I've never been in love."

"Well, she smiles at me whenever I walk in. She's beautiful, as is her name, Matilda, and she raves about each new piece, be it a chest or table that I've built. After her Mister Harris and I set it in place, she always walks over and tells me I'm an artist."

"I don't think that means nothing. I say the same things about your furniture," I replied.

He bowed his head in defeat but kept sanding the knob he was holding.

"The next time I go up there, I'll ask you to cut some roses from Ma's garden. You can make a bouquet, and I'll carry it to her. Do you think she will like that?" he asked.

"For certain she would. And be nice to her pa if you meet him, and to Mister and Missus Harris. But I guess they like you because they pay money for your furniture."

I sat and watched my uncle work for a bit, pondering him as a married man. I could not quite envision it because he still frequented saloons with my pa and still was inclined to get into brawls. Then I remembered that Pa was a married man, so I realized I knew nothing about getting wed. Nevertheless, in July Uncle Jeremy asked me to cut flowers for his trip to the inn. He placed them on the wagon seat next to him as he rode away, a newly hewn bench loaded in the back of the wagon.

"Did Matilda like the flowers you brought her?" I asked at breakfast the next morning.

His face flushed. "Yes," he answered, and went back to eating.

"Who's Matilda?" asked Grandma.

I knew right then that I should have waited to ask Jeremy about his friend. I'd clearly revealed information he had confided to me. Now the cat was out of the bag.

"She's a girl up at the inn. Likes the furniture I bring them," said Jeremy, trying to end the conversation.

Later, in the barn, I apologized to my uncle. "I'm sorry about breakfast. Was Matilda glad you brought her flowers?"

"Yes, she was," Jeremy said. "She even kissed me on the cheek, right in front of Missus Harris. Maybe I'll invite her to a church supper one week soon, though I wonder if they are Lutherans."

When school started in September, I was excited to return and see Miss Lerner again. She had gone to her parents' home in San Antonio for the summer, and I knew that she rented a room in the Harrell home when she was teaching school. Emily and I found our desks just as we'd left them in the spring.

I handed the book of Elizabeth Barrett Browning's poems to Miss Lerner.

"Thank you, Miss Lerner, for letting me borrow this for the summer. I took great joy in reading it and sharing with my sister."

"Well, may I ask? How did your sister feel about Miss Browning's poetry?" she asked.

I laughed so hard that the others in the room turned to look at me.

"She rolled her eyes, Miss Lerner," I said. I put my arms around her, hugged her. "I look forward to this year, Miss Lerner."

"As do I, Fidelia."

I walked back to my desk, wondering what it would feel like to be a school teacher, inspiring others in front of a classroom. I felt lured by thoughts of such a profession, yet doubted I would ever have the opportunity to go to a normal school that trained teachers. Miss Lerner had once told me she had studied in such a school in Massachusetts, before her family came to Texas. But I knew it was farming that ran in my family's blood. As I sat down at my desk, I perused the bookcases to see if there were any new authors or titles.

I remained diligent about my schoolwork and helping Ma and Grandma at home. Ma brought me to church over the religious holidays to help with celebrations, and I clung to the comraderies between the women, understanding why Ma felt comfortable there. The busier I kept myself with chores, with penning thoughts in my journal, and with sewing, the less often grief would find its hold on me.

CHAPTER 36

Uncle Jeremy's interest in Matilda had made him happier than I'd seen him in a long time. But my earlier instincts turned out to be correct, as revealed one day in late September when he came home with another black eye.

I saw him walk into the barn, before anyone else had seen him. But the story he told surprised even me.

"Yep. Got in another fight. You won't believe what happened. It was Seth. That damned, no-good conniver," said Jeremy.

"Seth? He is still 'round here?" I said.

"Well, he is. And he got himself a job at the inn taking care of the horses, a job for Mister Harris. Then he had the nerve to ask Mister Harris for permission to court Matilda. Mister Harris spoke with Matilda's pa and gave permission to Seth. Can you believe that?"

"No, but I did see that fella as a charmer. When he worked here, he had a way of getting what he wanted, including trouble. Did he give you the black eye?"

"Yeah. I confronted him when I found out about Matilda, and it ended up with us rolling around and punching each other in the barn. I'm sure he's going to tell Matilda."

"I guess you should have asked first, for permission to court Matilda. But, Uncle Jeremy, I think that Seth will get himself into trouble before it's all over. Yet I think you best stop fighting or you'll both be in trouble."

Jeremy stared at me, startled by my boldness. "Dammit, Fidelia, you're probably right. You sound like Grandma. Besides, I'm not marriage material and don't need no darn women to badger me." He looked at me. "You excluded, Miss McCord."

Whenever I found sadness intruding into my thoughts, I turned to my journal. I was only thirteen years old, but on the inside I felt so much older. Some days I'd envision my future as an old spinster eking out a life of despair.

I recalled the pastor's words. I remember him telling me I was not alone, so I felt filled with purpose and tried to remain steadfast with my pen. Grandpa had bought me two more leather books since he gifted me the first journal. Kept me supplied with ink. I filled the pages with my feelings, my desires, my sadness. And then I wrote poetry about sweet Audrey. Oh, how I missed her.

Mayfly

Red-haired spirit
so beloved, an aunt
who grasped each day
anew yet so soon gone.

She grabbed the ring.
She sang the moon
and danced with fireflies

headstrong, pure.

Her headstone etched
Loving daughter.
The worms now feast
all day long.

As October rolled to an end and the men had finished harvesting crops, I joined Grandpa on the back porch as the cicadas sang and the sunlight faded to dark. We sat in silence for a while, until Grandma came out to deliver a glass of cold lemonade to us and then vanished back indoors. The lantern flickered in the barn as Uncle Jeremy toiled in his workshop.

"Fidelia," Grandpa said. "I don't know what we would do without you. You and Emily are the light of youth left in our home."

He extinguished his pipe. I said nothing. *What was there to say?*

"You, dear girl, are the McCords' cherished gift. The promise of our future. Whatever you bring us, be it grandchildren or poetry or a good meal, we will be blessed."

"Thank you, Grandpa," I said. "I won't, with certainty, disappoint you, for I want to be just like you."

The moonlight revealed the hint of a smile on his face, and we sat quiet amidst the cicada songs of a country evening until we rose for bed.

In January, Grandma baked another ginger cake to celebrate my turning fourteen. Ma had made me a lovely scarlet cotton dress, ruffled at the buttoned bodice, that fit my figure and I felt like a lady wearing it. It was almost too pretty to wear to school and maybe a bit too bold for church, but I loved it.

In early February, on a cool and sun-filled Saturday after my chores, wearing my worn gray dress, I saddled and mounted Trapper and rode out to the cave. I should have told Grandpa I was going, but he would not have been happy, so I told Uncle Jeremy that I was going to the creek and would not be gone long. I had learned my lesson about being alone in the wild.

I found the cave quickly, but it looked different. It was overgrown and invisible, through the brush, to the human eye. I had forgotten to bring a lantern.

I'd not returned to this place since I'd almost died here. Filled with an odd hesitation, I sat on my horse. There were both precious memories and devastating ones. Maybe I should not go into the cave, the sanctuary, but walk away and leave it a tomb. Naught but a memory in honor of a friend. But the quietude and shelter of it beckoned me.

I pulled the moss and branches back and listened, making sure no animal had taken refuge inside, then I felt my way through the darkness to the room. As always, it was lit from above, more so because the trees were barren in winter. I sat in the middle of the room and, though I missed Rosa's presence, I thought of Emily. I should have brought her with me, so she could see the cave, but it was solitude that called me to come.

Memories of laughter echoed through the cave. It was here, when Rosa and I came together, that we laughed about our dreams and misdeeds. Oh, how I missed her. But our sanctuary was a place to be respected, for it held danger as well as respite. I rose to leave, finding my way out.

When the sun hit my eyes, blinding me for a moment, I thought I saw a shadow. It was Grandpa, sitting on his horse next to Trapper.

"You didn't think I wouldn't check on you, did you?" he said. "Jeremy said you'd come out here."

I smiled and mounted my horse, and we rode home in a carefree silence.

CHAPTER 37

It was a Saturday morning, in late February of the year I'd turned fourteen, when my morning chores were done, and the skies held a heavy fog. The scene was eerie, but I loved the foggy days, the veil of mist that conjured imaginary figures. The thick fog blurred everything before me as I pushed myself back and forth on the outside swing, breaking through the grounded clouds, when a movement caught my eye. Maybe a deer. Or Bear. But no, the shadow moved closer, like a ghost approaching, until I saw a horse moving toward the house, toward me. As the horse neared, I saw it carried a man, a man unfamiliar to me.

The man slowed his horse when he noticed me on the swing.

"G'day, Delia." The voice sounded familiar, but the man was not. "You now a woman, but I still know you."

I almost fainted. It was the voice of Gray Feather, but he looked different. Like a white man.

I jumped off the swing and stood still, muddled. "You have changed," I said. "You look different, Gray Feather."

"You think white man in Texas would not shoot an Indian? I traveled down here to Austin City with white men. They have gone to the city, but I wear white man's clothes."

He removed his hat and his braid fell down his back as it used to. I saw Grandpa coming out of the house to greet this stranger, whom I now knew was not a stranger after all.

I walked toward Gray Feather as he dismounted his gray mare.

"I never thought I would see you again. It so fills my heart to see you," I said.

"And mine to see you," he replied as Grandpa stood watching us, as muddled as I had been a few moments ago.

"Gray Feather!" said Grandpa. "I never expected to see you in Texas." Grandpa reached out to shake Gray Feather's hand, and they did so heartily.

"I did never believe I would be at Texas," Gray Feather said. He laughed and stopped suddenly, turned serious. "But I do come with sad news."

We both looked at him. I knew right then that Grandpa and I had the same thoughts—that we wanted no more bad news.

"Edmund has died. The reason I have come."

"Let's go inside. You can tell us, and we can feed you. I would surmise that you are hungry," said Grandpa.

"I am," responded Gray Feather.

The men sat at the table as Grandma, Ma, and I prepared dinner and set the table. Gray Feather told the tale of Edmund's demise. He had taken a bad fall in the mountains when collecting some traps. His leg became infected, and he died in his home a week later. His sister had come to nurse him, and Gray Feather was there.

"He is buried in Kansas City," said Gray Feather.

"I think your friend Edmund is one of the unluckiest fellows I've ever met," said Grandpa.

The door opened, and Pa and Jeremy stumbled in. They'd been gone into the city since Thursday night.

"Who the hell is this?" said Pa, yet a bit queasy from the rye he'd likely been drinking.

"Mind your manners, son!" said Grandpa.

"It is Gray Feather, John, and you will sit here and be courteous to him as we would to any guest. He's come to bring news of Edmund's death."

"Been dead to me since I left him in the woods in Missouri," said Pa, and he stumbled to his room as Jeremy stumbled up the stairs. I shook my head, embarrassed by my father, as Ma and Grandma apologized to our guest.

It did not escape my notice that Gray Feather was careful to follow our customs as he feasted with us, but he clearly was hungry, ravenous after his long journey. Ma served him a second plate for she, too, had clearly noticed his hunger. When we finished our meal, Ma took Gray Feather to the barn, where there was a pallet that would allow our friend to rest. I followed her with a water basin and set it on the small table near the bedding.

"You know I choose creeks for wash," said Gray Feather. A hint of a grin lit his face.

"I know, but for this moment it is too far. I will take you there tomorrow," I said. He nodded.

I saw the grimace on Ma's face and followed her back to the house.

"You are becoming too grown to accompany a man alone in the woods. Or to any place, Fidelia," said Ma as we entered the kitchen.

"But he is my friend, Ma."

"I know. But you heard what I said."

"Then Grandpa can go with us," I said. I stood straight, my chin held high.

"Or your grandpa can take him. You have chores, and

there is mending we have promised Missus Harrell," said Ma.

When I went inside, I walked straight to my desk, pulled out my journal, and dipped my silver Levy nib into the black ink.

> Edmund is now with my Aunt Audrey, joined for eternity with the woman he pined for. She is in his embrace at last. I can almost hear the echo of my aunt's laughter, as it had once echoed in the forest, and I pray she is garbed in the beautiful pink dress. Whom I pray to, I am not sure, for God has again taken another. In my head, I hear Pastor Wieland's words: *We all die.*
>
> There is yet a joy within my chest at the surprise of Gray Feather's visit. He is here with us. I never dreamed I would see him again, and I wish he could stay forever, but that is certainly foolish, for he would not be welcomed in Texas, seen by white men as a depraved enemy. Gray Feather has not yet revealed his plans, but I will revel in his company while he is here.

At breakfast the next morning, Grandpa and Gray Feather were not present.

"Where is Grandpa?" I asked Grandma.

"He took Gray Feather to the creek this morning," she

said. "Our guest asked to bathe at the creek."

I caught Ma's eyes as she glanced in my direction. I glared.

As I cleared the dishes into the wash pan, Grandpa and Gray Feather walked in. In minutes, Ma set a plate of bacon, biscuits, and eggs in front of the two men, and I poured each some hot coffee.

"Thank you. G'day, Fidelia. And Emily," said Gray Feather, looking toward me and then my sister. "Your grandfather has taken me to your creek. So near your farm."

"Yes. And sometimes Grandpa and I fish in the river, the Colorado. Such bounty there. Will you be here long enough to go with us?" I asked.

"No, not here long. My friends, who bring me to Austin City, made provisions for me to ride north with the stagecoach to Dallas. I wish to stay two days more, if your kindness will allow."

"What will you do in Dallas?" I asked.

"Fidelia, let the man eat his breakfast," said Grandpa.

"Yes, sir. I am sorry," I said.

Gray Feather took a gulp of his coffee, and Grandma was coming with more.

"All is good. I will go from Dallas on to Kansas. I go home to my tribe near the Verdigris River. My family."

I sat down at the table and sat with the men in silence. When the men rose, Ma told me to wash my hands.

"Here is the mending that must be done today," said Ma. She laid three dresses and a shirt on the blue chair.

Grandpa was about to show Gray Feather the barn and our fields, soon to be plowed for planting. But instead, Gray Feather turned to address all of us.

"Pardon me, Mister McCord, but I have come to Texas for reason I must share."

"Go on, Gray Feather," said Grandpa.

"I have come here to bring not just news of Edmund's death. I make promises to Edmund before his death. After the dinner, I will share these wishes then."

We all stood in silence. Dumbfounded. What could Edmund possibly have asked? Finally, Grandpa broke the silence.

"Then we will have a family meeting after dinner today," said Grandpa. "Let's go." He placed his hand on Gray Feather's shoulder and they left the house. In the ensuing quiet, I was filled with curiosity, but I pulled my shawl around my shoulders and gathered my sewing kit and the mending to the porch to work in the light.

CHAPTER 38

Grandma had made a stew for dinner, which warmed all of us on a chilly February day. I tried not to eat quickly, for I was eager to hear what Gray Feather would share with us but knew finishing early would only enrich my anxiety as I sat in wait. Even Pa had joined us, and though he said little, he was polite. Grandma's resolute gaze toward her son was potent.

"Now that we eat together, forgive me a moment. I have a bundle I must take from my horse," said Gray Feather, and he left the house. Grandma returned the big pot of stew to the stove, for she never allowed anyone to eat a cold meal.

Gray Feather returned with a long-rolled cowhide that he proceeded to unroll, and there lay three fine rifles, gleaming with rubbed oils.

"Edmund loved his guns, this one from war with Mexico." He picked up the gun Edmund had carried all those years ago when he'd visited us, and he handed it to my Grandpa.

"He was always grateful for kindness your family showed him, in spite of his faux pas with Miss Audrey. He tell me he wants you to have these guns. And these two carved boxes, for Missus Mariah and Missus McCord."

He handed the boxes to Ma, who gave one of them to Grandma. Ma ran her fingers over the intricate carving.

"Gray Feather, this is most generous of you," said Grandpa.

"No. Not me. Gift from Edmund."

"Yes, I understand. But you have traveled all this way. We do not feel deserving," said Grandpa.

"Edmund said you most deserve. Beside your kindness, he love your daughter like he love the land, the rivers, the air he breathe. My friend's love for Miss Audrey bring me to the last gift."

Gray Feather opened a small wooden box and lifted from it a ring.

"This is for you, Fidelia."

He handed me the ring. I sat in a chair and turned the ring over and over, gazing at the bold red garnet with large facets that reflected the sunlight. The ring was dressed in intricate gold, and it was vivid yet delicate, just like my aunt.

"For ring he bartered his furs, for Audrey, when he came to Texas to ask for marriage. He held it all these years, but never find another lady to match the love for your aunt," said Gray Feather, looking directly to me.

"For your kindness to him, to me, Fidelia, he wanted you to have this ring. He knew how much you loved your aunt, how you miss her." He handed me the box that had held the ring.

"Thank you." I didn't know what else to say, and my words trembled. I thought how beautiful this ring would have looked on Audrey's finger. I wondered what I should do with such a treasure. I could not wear this. I placed the ring back in the box.

"Grandma, is there a safe place you can keep this until I am old enough to wear it?" I asked, handing the box to her.

"Yes, dear," said Grandma.

"It is so beautiful, Gray Feather," I said. I wanted to hug him, but I knew that was not his custom, so I smiled and nodded.

"And for Emily, I have a beaded pouch. From Osage." He handed the pouch to my sister. "My friend was steadfast the ring go to you, Miss Delia."

"I will make you a jewelry chest," Jeremy said to me.

I nodded at Gray Feather, then smiled at Jeremy. Grandma took the ring from the box and showed it to Ma, who turned it as I had. Marveled at it.

Gray Feather spent much of the afternoon working with Jeremy in his workshop and with Grandpa, who made some fence repairs, brushed the horses, and freed them into the fenced pasture. When I was not busy with chores and when the mending was done, I shadowed my friend.

In the evening, Gray Feather sat on the porch with Grandpa and me, Emily swinging beneath the oak tree as Bear ran around her. We all watched the fireflies, and as if God held our happiness in His hand, a falling star flashed across the dark sky.

In the morning, our guest arrived late to breakfast. He shared that he had gone to the creek to wash, to pray, as I had remembered him doing in the Missouri woods.

"You happy here?" asked Gray Feather to no one in particular.

"We are, most of us. Our losses were great when we first arrived, and there was a year of bad drought when our crops failed," said Grandpa. "But our profits are now good and there's land to be had. John is applying for a grant near the river."

"So, you will be returning to the forests in Missouri? To trapping?" asked my pa. I was surprised that Pa had engaged in conversation with our friend.

"No. I will go to Kansas. To my family. As I remember, few trees in Kansas as well. But no enemy tribes in Kansas like Osage have in Texas and Oklahoma."

I trembled. Before I knew it, I felt the tears on my cheek. I could tell my family was watching me as I rose and walked up the stairs. I could hear the whispers at the table as I reached the top of the steps.

In my room I poured water into my basin and splashed some on my face, then raised the window to welcome fresh air and the sounds of an early work day. I was sitting on my bed when Ma walked in the room.

"Are you well, Fidelia?" she asked.

"Yes, Ma. I'm sorry. I was startled to hear those words, Gray Feather's words about enemy tribes, and remember how my friend met her end. Feelings just sank into my stomach like a weight. So unexpected," I replied.

Ma took my hand and squeezed it. She understood.

"Mama, I want to spend some time with Gray Feather before he leaves. Today, if I can. When will the stage go north again?"

"He told us tomorrow. He will meet up with the stagecoach tomorrow and be going north."

"I will miss him. But I had never thought I would see him again, and now he is here," I said.

"I know, dear. I know."

CHAPTER 39

It was mid-afternoon, and I wrapped my shawl about my shoulders and pinned it, then grabbed the blue folded blanket on the shelf. I walked out to the big oak tree and spread the blanket so I could read in the shaded sunlight. Gray Feather, as far as I knew, was still out in the fields with Grandpa, and I didn't know what had been said after I left the table so suddenly that morning.

It was the Sabbath, and Ma had gone off to church with Emily. I had to return to school tomorrow and would not even be here to say goodbye to my friend. I picked up the book of essays I had borrowed from school and began reading when I noticed a shadow fall across the blanket. It turned to find Gray Feather, and he sat on the blanket across from me, watching me as I lay down my book.

"I hear of your sadness, Fidelia. Your friend, your sisters. Look at you. Almost a woman. But you a strong woman, like I tell you in the forest, when you only a girl."

I looked at him, disbelieving. "So many are gone, Gray Feather. Lost to this place called heaven. How can I be so strong?"

"You, the strong one. In your heart."

"Like a bear?" I asked, my voice holding a derisive quality, which I immediately regretted.

"A bear?"

"Yes. Remember, you told me, in the Ozark Mountains,

that I was strong like a bear?"

"Ah. Yes, that is what I said." He paused for a moment. "You know bears noble. You are much like a bear, for they are . . . what is your word . . . curious, and thoughtful. They are smart and love family, like a tribe. This is like you."

My back straightened. It was odd how Gray Feather always made me feel just as he described me. As if he had a special power.

"Yet my friend Rosa and family are gone. It leaves an emptiness, Gray Feather."

"Ah, but no. You are now all. You are your little sisters and you are Fidelia, all together. And you are Audrey. You are not alone, my friend. You are today greater than you have been before."

"How?"

"Their spirits always walk with you. When the sun shines, the moon glow at night. Beside you, in your heart?" He put his hand over his own heart.

"And Rosa?"

"Yes. I hear about Rosa. Not all Indians good Indians, Delia. And not all white men good men."

He sat silent, letting me absorb his words.

"But look. Over there," said Gray Feather, pointing toward the trees. "See her?"

I looked and looked, seeing nothing.

"You may not always see her, but she is here with you. Rosa is part of you, makes you who you are. She will see the world through your eyes, feel the wind in hair. You now see the world through her eyes. You will command her courage. Be stronger."

I just stared at him, and he at me. I thought back to the year when I was only eight years old, the moments when I felt the spirit of my aunt Audrey within me, moments when I saw things around me through my dead aunt's eyes. I shuddered. Gray Feather watched me in silence, as if he could see my thoughts. We sat quietly until a mockingbird interrupted our silence with a melody, along with the chirping sparrows, as if the birds awaited our reply. Gray Feather turned to me, as if that little mockingbird had spoken directly to him.

"Let us just sit here in the winter sky, and let the little birds sing."

As we sat, I saw my friend at ease, listening to the birdsong, but I knew he had counted on the chorus of my thoughts. Gray Feather's words echoed in my head, as he knew they would. I took in a deep breath and broke our silence.

"I believe what you say. So, your friend Edmund was not alone either, was he?" I looked into Gray Feather's eyes, searching. "Audrey was always with him, wasn't she?"

"I tell you are smart girl. But you are more smart than I ever know. The god of the sky, my *Wa-kon-ta*, and your god from the Bethlehem . . . they will carry you ever in the wind and will light your path with sunrays and stars. No matter what sorrows come, you never be alone, my friend, for we are all part of the great one who gives life. Just as I walk with my tribe, my tribe here on land, in Kansas, everywhere . . . even those returned to the soil in Missouri. They are with me each day, with each step I hear them, whispers . . . in the wind, in the heart, in how my hand moves, in my thoughts."

My heart filled with my friend's words. Words that gathered and merged into a belief like the cotton I would weave into lace. Like a flock of geese who gather in formation beneath the clouds of winter with trust in their destination. The geese, all together. Another tribe. My friend's words resonated in a lightness that filled my chest.

The two of us sat silent again, and Grandma walked toward us from the house, carrying two mugs of hot tea to warm us on the cool day.

"Are you having a good visit?" she asked us.

"Yes," said Gray Feather. "Your granddaughter such a smart and brave girl."

Grandma smiled.

"No. A young woman," he said.

"Yes. She is. She has grown up so much, too soon in so many ways." And with those words, Grandma looked at me with a serious face, as if she saw me anew.

"When Mariah returns from the church, we will fix dinner. And I will prepare you a package of food to take with you tomorrow," she said to Gray Feather, then turned toward the house.

We visited until the sun was leaning to the west. I had never heard Gray Feather, a man of great thought and few words, speak as much as on that day. In my heart, I believed it to be because of our friendship and of a certain knowledge that we'd not see each other again.

Gray Feather asked if I would read aloud an essay from the book I held. Afterwards, I told him about my friend Rosa and her family, about Abe, and about the cave. I told him how I had almost died there twice, and he pressed me to be more careful. I promised that I would.

Ma and Emily came up the path in the buggy, and Emily waved and yelled at us. Gray Feather and I rose, and he helped me fold the blanket before we walked to the house.

I stayed near Gray Feather for the rest of the day, knowing I would not see him after I left the next morning. Our supper was wholesome for a winter meal. Grandma had snapped a chicken and roasted it with onions. She'd gathered canned tomatoes and corn and stewed them together, and Ma had baked a cake with chocolate, a special treat.

I sat on the porch with Grandpa and Gray Feather as night wrapped the farm, the moon almost full and brilliant. Jeremy joined us when he finished his work in the barn. It was the next morning that I dreaded. Saying goodbye.

But the morning came nonetheless. I had thrown my cotton work dress over my chemise to go out and milk the dairy cow. She was edgy and impatient with me that morning, or maybe it was me who was high-strung, and I had to keep chasing my sister's cats away from the milk pail. The bucket was full when I saw Gray Feather take his horse from the stall.

"I must say farewell to you this morning. I am off to school," I said.

He walked toward me, his horse following. "Never farewell. Remember what I told you. I, too, am always with you. You with me."

I wanted to hug him, but thinking it might be awkward, I instead pulled the stone from my pocket, the small chertz I'd found in Missouri.

"Here. This is for you, so you will remember me. It is an arrowhead that I found in the Missouri forest. In the Ozarks."

He could not hold back his smile.

"You return Osage weapon to me? I honored. I accept with thanks. I will cherish, but I not need this to remember you. You will be gone when I return from the creek to depart. But you always here," he said, putting his hand to his chest. I did the same, and he turned to leave. He did not see the tears in my eyes.

CHAPTER 40

April was filled with rains and work, but one morning I came into the barn for my chores and heard a strange noise from the horse stalls. I walked back toward the horses and heard snoring. I thought it was probably one of the animals, but I opened a stall to find Grandpa sound asleep in the hay. Beside him lay a brand-new black foal. He had been up all night helping the gray mare birth new life.

The small foal looked at me, then teetered toward the mare to nurse. I felt so filled with love for my grandpa, seeing him asleep. I left him to rest and walked back to my chore, reminding myself to tell Grandma where I'd found him.

In May, the fireflies were flitting through the darkening sky on a hot spring night as I sat on the porch, rocking in Grandpa's chair. Emily and Bear were near the barn chasing the flickering lights. Grandpa walked out the kitchen door, tamping tobacco into his pipe, and I jumped up and moved to the bench. He sat in his chair and lit his pipe, drawing breaths to keep it lit. He looked toward me.

"It's done," he said.

I looked at him. I wasn't sure what he meant.

"Abe and Reka are moving here to our farm. I managed a deal with Hans by purchasing the two large fields nearest our farm. Two of the slaves come to me, and he agreed to take the third slave to his farm and give him his freedom in precisely one year. The profits we make from those extra fields will allow me to pay Abe a bit and provide them shelter. Does that work?"

I jumped up from the bench and ran to hug my grandpa. "I love you, Grandpa."

"I know you do, dear, and I love you more than you know. I kept talking to Hans, a hard fella to deal with. When he sets his mind to something, I found it's hard to bend it. It didn't hurt that the young Mister Brandt wants to move back home to his own plantation."

"He's leaving?" I asked.

"Probably after the harvest. He finally gave in to my proposal when I told him how much this meant to you and to his own mother. All the circumstances came together to get what you wanted, Fidela."

"Abe will work here? He'll be a free man? And his wife too?" I asked.

"Yes, they will. But this is still a slave state, so we won't be discussing their free status with people. Abolitionists, free-staters, are not at all welcome in Texas. As for Abe and Reka's freedom, it's on the papers. We know it; they know it. That's enough for now."

I nodded.

"There is bit of information that Hans shared with me. I am hesitant to discuss Rosa's death, but I believe it is something you'd want to know."

I didn't know what to say, but a quiver ran up my back.

"Hans received a letter from an authority in

Fredericksburg that Rosa did not die at the hands of the Indians. It appeared she had escaped from their campsite, and in her journey, probably at night, she'd fallen from a cliff along the Seco Creek. It is believed that the fall caused her death."

My eyes watered, but my heart filled. I knew this was my friend's spirit. She was bold and determined.

"Grandpa?"

"Yes, Fidelia?"

"She denied the killers of her parents, didn't she? She ran towards home at risk to herself, and doing such, she joined her ma and pa," I said. My voice trembled.

"That is a keen way to see it, like that, granddaughter. And I believe it to be the truth."

I sat on the bench, imaginings of Rosa's last hours running wild in my head. I looked up at Grandpa and saw him watching me.

"I can't wait to see Abe and Reka at our farm. How soon will they come? Where will they live?" I asked, not wanting to speak any more of death, but of Abe's future.

"We shall all raise a cottage for them, as soon as they can come," he replied.

He puffed on his pipe, and like the spirals of smoke, I twirled on the steps. Emily joined us and we twirled together.

"I will be praying that our crops are bountiful this year so that we can build that cottage behind the barn," said Grandpa.

"I love you, Grandpa."

Emily mimicked me. "I love you, Grandpa."

Today was a good day. Rosa would be proud of me. Abby, oh, dear Abby, would be beside herself.

CHAPTER 41

By fall of 1854, Grandpa and Jeremy had fenced in the new acreage. The harvest was coming to an end, and behind the barn the frame of a new cottage stood ready to finish. With all four of the men working, it would be finished in a couple of weeks.

In addition to helping with the mending and alterations, Emily and I spent the cooler days making some dresses for Reka. I cannot say how delighted I was to have Abe and Reka near us, almost part of our larger family. Reka helped Ma and Grandma with chores that had often fell to them, combing seeds from the cotton, melting fats and pouring tapers, and churning the butter. For all of Reka's help, Grandma often sent a meal out to the couple, though Grandpa had installed a stove in their cottage, finished before the chill of winter came.

Without my Rosa, I spent more time with my sister. I told Emily about Rosa's family, how her ma and pa met and fell in love, how they danced in the kitchen. I told her about our horse rides with Missus Brandt, and how we would sometimes sneak away. And, finally, I told Emily about the secret cave. She wanted to go.

"Fidelia, I want to see it. You said it was a sanctuary, so we can share it now," she said.

"Em, Rosa and I almost drowned there. And then I almost died from fever before Pa found me."

"But you loved it there," wailed Emily.

I paused. "Yes, I did, Em. But dangers came with it. Maybe in the spring, after winter. Maybe on a sunny day I will show it to you," I said with hesitancy. Emily was now a girl of twelve, her golden curls falling around her shoulders. She would be a beautiful woman one day not so far away, but she was still so full of innocence. She preferred afternoons at the spinning wheel or stitching by the lantern with Grandma in the evening, whereas I loved fishing with Grandpa on early mornings.

Grandpa tried hard to keep my spirits up, but there were still some nights when I would cry as I thought of Rosa. Nightmares ensued when I imagined beautiful Missus Brandt running for her life, pulling her daughter with her after seeing her husband pierced by an arrow. No one saw what happened, but these imaginings often stole my sleep.

On those nights when I cried, Emily would crawl into my bed and snuggle close, her hand on my shoulder. My sister had such a happy nature that I would sometimes hold my sadness inside to spare her.

On a cool October evening, following one of my sleepless nights, I sat down at my desk with the lantern lighting my blank paper. My body was tired, but my mind filled. The flame from the light created wavering shadows on the page, reminding me that my loved ones were near. I had thought of Rosa throughout the day as I had through the sleepless night before, and now I was reminded of her presence in the room. I remembered Gray Feather's words to me, and suddenly my pen filled the page.

Sanctuary

is not a promise,
not a place,
but a jewel one finds
when God's
sweet fingers lace,
where it sings
from the smallest nest,
where His grace
reels in the stillness
of the pond
and sends the wind
through my hems
and carries the clouds
to dance at my song.

Sanctuary is the world
revealed through the eyes
of my friend,
now gone,
through a walk
in the woods of night
where the new moon
glows bright,
and ancestors gather
and exalt the living.

Sanctuary is a strong
stitch on a 'broidered
sleeve to charm
a glance and a hand

holding tight to mine,
a cool palm, tender,
on a fevered brow,
and the endless covenant
of a sacred vow.

My sister walked up behind me and asked to see my poem, so I read it to her. She smiled and had a look of insight that I had never remembered seeing on her face.

"Fidelia. Tomorrow we should help Reka make some curtains for her cottage," said Emily.

"Do we have some fabrics?" I asked. "That we can use?"

"Ma bought some at the general store in Austin. Let's go ask," she said, and off we went, seeking fabrics to embellish Abe and Reka's new home. The following day we brought Reka over to help choose her favorites. She was so grateful, filled with glee, and she told us she'd never before had such lovely cloth or curtains.

With the help of Abe about the farm, Pa seemed less stressed, less angry, but the free time seemed to give him license to spend more time away from home. Though I worried about Ma being distressed, she seemed happy being involved at the church, helping Grandma with canning, and doing the mending they took in for fees. Sometimes I'd earn a bit of money with my tatting, making lace for neighbor's dresses and selling finished pieces at the market.

I still remember the day I cut the lace from the ruffle on that old yellow dress from Arkansas, a dress long outgrown by my sister, the fabric frayed. I stitched the cherished lace onto a new chemise Ma had sewn for my sister. I always got the new dresses; Emily would get them later. My sister still helped with the spinning, and Reka often helped Ma dye the threads and yarns. Reka would comb the cotton seeds out before spinning and help Ma mix the dyes from the tree barks and blooms, even onion skins, providing me with beautiful embroidery threads.

Emily and I went out of our way to help Ma, and we worked together to make her a beautiful new cloak of boiled wool dyed a dark red, complete with embroidered borders on the cuffs and hood. Ma loved her new cloak, and when she tried it on, I did not miss the look on Pa's face as he watched her. My ma was a lovely woman whose beauty was often concealed beneath her work dress and fatigue, and now I saw how the deep red color revealed a glow in her eyes. There was a gaiety in her face, a light that I had not seen in years. My heart skipped a beat. Maybe I only needed new dreams to ease away my sadness. Dreams of my ma and pa walking hand in hand again, as I had once seen them strolling beside our Indiana cornfield.

I stood one morning, in the workshop, watching Jeremy finish a dining table for Abe's new home. He worked with expertise in sanding the wood smooth and adding a dark stain, then rubbed the wood with oil so that it would withstand daily use.

"I heard a young couple, recently wed, bought the farm next door, the Brandt farm," he said.

"Do they have slaves?" I asked.

"I believe Father said they did have two or three."

This made me sad, but I was happy for Abe and Reka, especially happy because Reka now carried a baby due in late spring, and the new dresses we'd made her no longer fit. Grandma said she would show Reka how to change the waistline.

CHAPTER 42

I was a different person as I rode to school after that Christmas in 1854. Even Miss Lerner noticed.

"You seem changed, Fidelia," she said to me.

In the afternoon, as I rode back home, I was filled by sorrows and a great joy, miraculously at the same time.

After supper and after the kitchen was cleaned, I sat at my desk, dipping the silver-steel nib into the black ink.

28 December, 1854

In the past year my grandpa freed two slaves and secured the promise for another. If ever a man stood tall and kept his covenants, it is my Grandpa. And my friend Gray Feather has surely arrived at his home in Kansas. This night, as I sit here in the flickering light of a candle, in a quiet room where I watch the dancing of light from the fireflies out the window, my Indian friend stands beside me. Still. I look forward to comings and goings, beside me, of my aunt, my friend Rosa, my baby sisters. Oh, and dear, sweet Abby. Such presence will lift me as if I were winged. I am certain.

I miss Rosa's mother, even Mister Brandt. Missus Brandt, who embraced me as if I were family. I will always remember the music of her country, Mexico, and watching her dance with her husband in the dimness of kitchen candlelight, looking into each other's eyes. Yes, just as Gray Feather said. I will now see the world through their eyes.

I do not know what my future holds; it is a story yet unfolded. I hope for more schooling but am certain that is not to be. I know Pa will need help building a cabin when he finds his land. I've learned from my friend Gray Feather that I am to stand tall and do what needs done.

I am filled with wonder at the courage of my family and my friends. I will always miss Gray Feather, for his wise words came like rivers and clouds and prayers. I will always feel his presence, as he taught me. For isn't my hand now guided by all those who are gone, just as my eyes see the world through theirs?

I yet think of Aunt Audrey often. Sometimes I wish I had her reckless spirit, so full of life. I am certain that Pa would say I am reckless. My memories of my aunt taught me great lessons, lessons that Gray Feather had also spoken. To live each day as if it is the only day. And secondly, Audrey taught me to choose life's paths with such care, for there are consequences to every one.

My dearest Rosa, now with her family. God clearly has a plan, for I do feel my loved ones around me. To feel them in the stillness, like Gray Feather taught me. God's grace has saved my own life over and over again. Each river we crossed, each fever that passed, each foolish choice I made.

And now, here in these meadows, for all its ruggedness, I have come to love this farm. The fields of winter that radiate with blooms each spring. The cottonwoods and oaks. The swift storms that nourish the land and fill the creeks. Fishing in the grand river. Grandma and Grandpa always at my side, and now Abe and Reka. In spite of the laws and the shame of slavery, I am certain we are all family. Abby's bold spirit will walk beside and guide her great-grandchild. Oh, the vision of this in my head is so large!

And Ma. She needs me, and I know she needs Pa. My prayers for Pa have often gone unanswered, yet on that night he saved me in the cave, that night I knew he loved me. I pray one day he finds solace.

It is odd how I am so different than I was only one year ago. That lightness that came to me then, when I talked with my Osage friend . . . that lightness he bequeathed has only grown and is swelling. It makes me stand tall. Though he is miles down the road, his spirit raises me.

Though I have always loved the forests, I have come to love more the Texas skies filled with storm clouds lit by the sun, filled with the light and dark in life. I can see the future where the sun shines on me, and I will embrace what God has planned, for there's room in my heart for all of it.

Acknowledgments

This story began when I was invited to a book club in Cypress Creek, when this lovely group of ladies shared with me a wonderful Boston Colony meal to enhance our discussion of *A Thousand Stars* and, then, they discussed their interest in a nearby Texas log cabin. I found only basic information about the cabin, but eventually found that it was not built by the man it was named after, but by the man's father-in-law. And there the story began. I read through records and letters and wandered through cemeteries to find the story of a family that traveled to Texas from Illinois in 1847. Their losses were immense. It was this story of their daughter, Fidelia, that inspired my fictional story of Fidelia McCord. The life journeys of our early pioneers were filled with a perseverance beyond today's understanding. I am filled with admiration and a little bit of envy.

In bringing this story to the novel held in your hand, I thank Nick Courtright for his editorial guidance and ever-positive outlook in spite of my abundant questions. I was fortunate to have an outstanding proofreader who caught the glitches; I couldn't have finished this book without her. I thank Jenny Quinlan, at Historical Editorial, for her always-outstanding book cover design, for her ability to capture the story in an image. Many thanks to my beta readers and their feedback, and to my writing club as they listened to the words as this story developed. And I have to add thanks to my orthopedic surgeon, Dr. Tyler Goldberg, for giving me a new hip as the old one had me teetering in the midst of writing this novel.

I must confess that I've fallen in love with the characters in this book, which is a good thing, because Fidelia's story will continue. I've shared this story in spirited Fidelia's words, and she continues to speak to me.

For updates and more information, visit me at: sandrafox.murphy.com

IF YOU ENJOYED THIS STORY, PLEASE
LEAVE A REVIEW ON AMAZON OR GOODREADS.

Discussion Questions

1. How did Fidelia cope with the death of her beloved Aunt Audrey? With her grief?

2. What changed John McCord, Fidelia's father? How did this young girl see the differences, and how did it impact her and those around her?

3. How important was Grandpa in Fidelia's life? For the family?

4. Edmund Chouteau disrupted the family's journey through the Ozarks. How did the different characters in the story see the charming Edmund?

5. Discuss Mariah McCord's struggles. As the reader, do you feel you came to know Mariah, and, if not, why do you think she seemed distant from the reader?

6. Fidelia was drawn to Abby. What do you think intrigued young Fidelia and what did the young girl and the old woman bring to each other? How did young Fidelia envision slavery, and what do you believe motivated her views?

7. In an era when women were second-class and

children were to be seen and not heard, how did Fidelia negotiate her beliefs and opinions?

8. How were Fidelia and Rosa different from each other? How did their differences complement each other? What impact did the Brandt family have on Fidelia?

9. How did Uncle Jeremy fit into the family and how does it impact his behavior? His contributions?

10. Brushy Creek, as well as the pond and the river, are both solace and adventure for Fidelia, and for Grandpa. Describe.

11. Fidelia struggles, throughout the story, with faith. How does this change through the story, through her grief, through her friendships?

12. Describe the woman you imagine to be telling this story. What has she learned throughout her life journey? Who has influenced her along the way?

ABOUT ATMOSPHERE PRESS

Atmosphere Press is an independent full-service publisher for books in genres ranging from non-fiction to fiction to poetry, with a special emphasis on being an author-friendly approach to the challenges of getting a book into the world. Learn more about what we do at atmospherepress.com.

We encourage you to check out some of Atmosphere's latest releases, which are available at Amazon.com and via order from your local bookstore:

Mandated Happiness, a novel by Clayton Tucker
Transcendence, poems and images by Vincent Bahar Towliat
Time Do Not Stop, poems by William Guest
Adrift, poems by Kristy Peloquin
Dear Old Dogs, a novella by Gwen Head
Bello the Cello, a picture book by Dennis Mathew
Ghost Sentence, poems by Mary Flanagan
That Scarlett Bacon, a picture book by Mark Johnson
Makani and the Tiki Mikis, a picture book by Kosta Gregory
What Outlives Us, poems by Larry Levy
How Not to Sell, nonfiction by Rashad Daoudi
That Beautiful Season, a novel by Sandra Fox Murphy
What I Cannot Abandon, poems by William Guest
All the Dead Are Holy, poems by Larry Levy
Rescripting the Workplace, nonfiction by Pam Boyd

About the Author

Sandra Fox Murphy wrote her first novel in 2015 after retiring from the U.S. Geological Survey. She is intrigued by the journeys of our ancestors, and before writing *Let the Little Birds Sing*, she published *A Thousand Stars*, set in Rhode Island, and a Civil War tale called *That Beautiful Season*. Sandra finds that the history of early America begs for the stories of the characters, both real and imagined, to be told.

Born in Delaware and growing up as a USAF "brat," she eventually found her way to Texas where she graduated from The University of Texas at Austin. She has lived throughout the USA and on islands in both the Atlantic and the Pacific. She now resides in central Texas and dreams of living in Marfa.

Learn more at www.sandrafoxmurphy.com.

CPSIA information can be obtained
at www.ICGtesting.com
Printed in the USA
FFHW021813071218
49752801-54219FF